SHADOWS BEHIND THE SCENERY

MARY ANN NOE

Black Rose Writing | Texas

This is a work of fiction. Names, characters, businesses, places, events, and incidents are either the products of the author's imagination or used in a fictitious manner. Any resemblance to actual persons, living or dead, or actual events is purely coincidental.

ISBN: 978-1-68513-704-5
LIBRARY OF CONGRESS CONTROL NUMBER: 2025944547
PUBLISHED BY BLACK ROSE WRITING
www.blackrosewriting.com

Printed in the United States of America
Suggested Retail Price (SRP) $18.95

Shadows Behind the Scenery is printed in Gentium Book Basic

*As a planet-friendly publisher, Black Rose Writing does its best to eliminate unnecessary waste to reduce paper usage and energy costs, while never compromising the reading experience. As a result, the final word count vs. page count may not meet common expectations.

For the real Jim and Heather Hamilton,
and 60-plus years of friendship Across the Pond

PRAISE FOR
SHADOWS BEHIND THE SCENERY

"Mary Ann Noe deftly blends historical fiction, espionage, and theater in this tension-laden WWII tale, vividly capturing the hazards of wartime travel, the resilience of Londoners under siege, and the shadowy world of intelligence work."
–Cam Torrens, award-winning author of The Tyler Zahn suspense novels.

"*Shadows Behind the Scenery* is an enchanting read for lovers of historical fiction, theatre, and wartime intrigue. Noe's skillful storytelling and intimate knowledge of her subjects make this novel a standout, offering suspense, style, and a heartfelt tribute to two of theater's greatest legends."
–Niamh McAnally, The Writer on the Water, Author of *Stories of Place*

"In *Shadows Behind the Scenery*, the beloved acting duo of Alfred Lunt and Lynn Fontanne travels to England during the height of World War II, expecting to boost morale with their performances. However, what begins as a patriotic mission to entertain becomes a gripping story of the courageous adaptation of acting to espionage."
–Elaine Mary Griffin, author of *Shadows in the Pleasure Gardens*

"Mary Ann Noe's *Shadows Behind the Scenery* is a story full of action and suspense. I was particularly moved by the portrait of a Britain where courage in the service of patriotism was prized. I would recommend *Shadows Behind the Scenery* to anyone who is a fan of historical crime fiction."
–Lea O'Harra, Author of *Sayonara, My Sweet*

"Mary Ann Noe's tale of intrigue and deception paints a vivid and compelling picture of London leading up to 1944's crucial D-Day operation. Central to the story is legendary American acting duo Alfred Lunt and Lynn Fontanne who come to England to entertain the troops, and are recruited by a British agent for a foray into espionage. A "must"read."
–James Hamilton, British civil servant, retired

SHADOWS BEHIND THE SCENERY

~1~

If Lynn Fontanne were a nail biter, that's what she'd be doing. As it was, she was twiddling her fingers, when she wasn't twirling the ends of the ties on her cream silk blouse, pacing. Back and forth, back and forth, in front of the windows looking out on Central Park. Stopping occasionally to peer down the street. Frowning. Waiting. Waiting for the mail delivery with their travel documents from the Federal State Department, who insisted on miles of paperwork before giving permission to travel to London before the end of 1943. There was a war raging over there, after all.

The trees in the park across the street glowed orange and red, backlit by the afternoon sun. The day was mild, but misty, for October, and the bank of windows that graced the front of the brownstone were open, though the air was New York air, not the fresh vibrant air of Ten Chimneys in Wisconsin, the couple's summer estate. There, the air could be fragrant with cut clover or ripe with shades of manure. Either aroma delighted Alfred, Lynn's husband, the farmer-actor of the pair, though Lynn preferred the clover, or the roses planted along the side of the creamery. She stopped pacing and closed her eyes for a moment, hoping to be wafted off in her mind. This infernal waiting was grating on her nerves.

She reached around to tuck any escaped loops of hair back into the net snood holding the twist at her neckline. Finding none, the task at least kept her fingers occupied. Running her hands down from the center part, she smoothed out the already smooth dark hair framing her face. The grooming gave her a moment of quiet.

Her brief interlude was interrupted.

"What are you up to, Lynnie?" Alfred Lunt strode into the room, dapper as always in a burgundy smoking jacket and muted gray checked ascot.

"I'm waiting for the mail delivery," Lynn said, without deserting her post. So much for escape. She skated her hands down the front of her pencil-thin brown tweed skirt, a nervous habit she rarely allowed herself to indulge in. "Our papers should be here today. Why they didn't come earlier, I cannot fathom. We were assured–"

"Here he comes." Alfred, taller than she was by almost a head, was already at the window, craning to see farther down the sidewalk.

Lynn spun away and headed for the front door. "I can catch him as he comes up the steps. I'll be right back." In an instant, she was out into the foyer. She couldn't hear if Alfred had a rejoinder, as he sometimes did. He occasionally felt she was too impatient. She reached the door, flung it open and sent out her most dazzling smile. "I hope you have something for us today."

"Yes, ma'am. Always a lot for you." The mailman held out a sheaf of envelopes, which Lynn scooped up. He turned away, threw a wave over his shoulder and clattered down the outside steps.

Lynn didn't wait until he reached the bottom, but shut the door and hurried back to the living room and Alfred. She sat down on the couch and fanned the mail out on the cushion next to her. "I'm afraid to look, Alfred, we've been waiting so long."

Alfred joined her, knelt, and reached out to help her sort.

Lynn batted his hand away, but it was a gentle love tap. She pushed the envelopes around with one finger, seeking out one with the State Department seal and return address. She scowled, picked up the pile and began sifting, one at a time. "Nothing, Alfred. Nothing!" She flung the pile down on the couch.

Alfred shoved the mail aside and rose to sit beside her. He put his arm around her, and she sank into him. "I don't know why our papers haven't come yet either," he said.

"They promised!" Lynn was petulant. "We can't wait much longer. It's already October. Pretty soon, the Atlantic is going to be so stormy, the ships won't want to venture out." Not only that...she barely could think it, to say nothing of speaking it out loud...the German U-boats and Luftwaffe were still on the prowl. "If they don't let us get overseas soon, they may not give us permission at all. We've been down to Washington, what, twice now?"

"I suppose we could call and pester them some more," Alfred offered.

"I need to get to London, Alfred. For one thing, my sister is there, and I am concerned for her safety." Though Lynn left England more than twenty years before, her native country still held aspects of home.

"Antoinette's a strong woman. I'm sure we'd hear from her if she were in dire need. We've sent her plenty of packages, and every single one went through. So far, communication lines are open."

Lynn recognized Alfred's attempt to smooth over the situation. "I know, darling, I know. It's just so hard sitting on this side, waiting for permission. We have the best of intentions. Not just to get to Antoinette either. The anti-war play we'll mount is so very powerful. It will certainly give our audiences the heart to keep going in these terrible times."

"I'm glad we decided to shelve the comedy we were going to add."

Lynn chuckled. "When they told us what the props and costumes weighed for that play, and the space they took up, I remember their faces. 'Not possible!' they said. Adamant. So, yes, it was easier to keep only *There Shall Be No Night*." This was a play reprised from their wildly successful 1940 tour three years ago, before the United States was thrust into the war. A pacifist family forced to decide if they would defend their homeland from an invading army. Dark, powerful, and the perfect vehicle to play to an audience in just that state, to give them strength for what they were doing for England, for Europe, for the world.

Alfred patted her hand. "You are magnificent as the mother, especially when you have to allow your only child to join the military and fight for the homeland."

Lynn loved it when Alfred rained praise on her performances. She knew, however, that he was insecure in his own roles, even though he shone like the brightest star on stage. He always complained that he was "horrible, Lynnie, just horrible," and then would go on to catalog everything he thought went wrong. This went on for a couple of hours, while Lynn bolstered his ego, pointing out, quite rightly, that critics loved him, audiences loved him, even she loved him. He always settled down in the end.

Now, she looked up at him and said, "The father has an even deeper role, considering he finally gives up his pacifist stance when their son is killed and he realizes that some things simply must be fought for. I especially love how you deliver those lines." She lifted an arm in a graceful and dramatic gesture as she quoted, "'One dynamic race is on the march to occupy the earth's surface and rule it. When you have absorbed that huge conception, you will find that your own theories can be adjusted to it.' Simply superb, Alfred, simply superb."

"You're divine to say so, my dear. I–"

The doorbell interrupted their reminiscence.

"I'll get it," Alfred said, and rose to go to the door.

~2~

When Alfred came back, he was leading a man in a lightweight belted trench coat. His fedora was carried in one hand, and what looked like a wallet in the other.

Lynn rose to meet them, a bit dismayed at Alfred's lack of hospitality. The man, after all, still had his outerwear on. "Take his–"

Alfred interrupted her with a gesture. "This man is from the State Department."

Lynn's words froze on her lips, and she seemed incapable of producing any sounds at all. The only thing that moved was her arm, which seemed to stretch out all on its own, hand palm up, to accept, or maybe demand, his identification.

The man apparently understood her unspoken question. He unfolded his wallet and set it on her hand. "Agent Thompson, ma'am. George Thompson, Federal State Department."

Was this it? Lynn thought. Our savior with our papers? She was chilled inside. Why was the State Department here? The postal system was quite adequate in normal situations. Did this mean they were withdrawing their permission to leave the country? She begged any unseen force out there in the universe to not let that happen.

Taking a deep breath, she returned to her usual gracious self. "Please, have a seat." She indicated a chair. Taking Alfred's elbow, Lynn guided him to sit beside her on the couch, across from the agent. She realized she was still clutching his wallet. "So sorry, Agent..." She glanced down at the identification badge in the wallet. "Thompson. Agent Thompson." She closed the wallet and handed it over to him as he sat down and set his fedora on the floor beside him.

"Now, what's this all about?" Alfred asked. He seemed the picture of calm.

Lynn knew better. He was in actor mode. Though she too sat very still, she was vibrating inside. But she was far too polite, now that she had a real State Department official held captive in their living room, to display impatience.

The agent reached into an inner pocket and struggled a bit to extract what appeared to be a large manila envelope. "I'm just flabbergasted to meet you two. I've met plenty of bigwigs, but most of them are political folks. I've followed you two for forever." The envelope popped out of his pocket and he handed it to Alfred. "Your travel papers."

Lynn's uneasiness deflated like a spent balloon. Now, she was eager. "Go ahead, Alfred, open it," she urged.

Alfred unwound the string that secured the top, opened the flap and pulled out a sheaf of papers.

"Careful," Thompson said. "Your renewed passports are down in there too." He sat with his feet flat and his arms on his knees, folded hands in front of him. "Make sure you check that everything you need is there."

Alfred handed the pages, one by one, to Lynn. They perused each with as much care as they did a fresh script. There weren't many. One listing their contact people in England, one delineating their roles once in London, one cover letter assuring that the bearers had permission to enter a war zone, all embossed with the State Department seal. Alfred plunged his hand to the bottom of the envelope and drew out their passports. Those they also examined, checking that the information was correct, and that the facing page sported their most recent official photo.

"As you can see," Thompson said, appearing more as a voiceover than as a person-to-person conversation, "you're set to sail on the ship the *Stage Door Canteen* from Philadelphia next Friday."

Lynn's and Alfred's heads snapped to attention at that, their passports held motionless.

"*Stage Door Canteen?*" Alfred's voice went up an octave and boomed out.

Lynn started to laugh. She put her hands up to her mouth, but not to stifle the merriment, but to revel in it. "Alfred, I can't believe it! This is a very good omen."

Thompson looked confused for a moment. But then his face cleared. "Oh, right. That's what you two have been doing here in New York, haven't you, working at the Stage Door Canteen soldiers' club, feeding the men, dancing with them." That last with a glance and a smile at Lynn.

"All of those film and theater stars too, the big bands, every one of us volunteers." Alfred looked down at his wife with a sad smile. "We are sending the boys off to war."

"I know, Alfred." Lynn set her hand on his thigh. "But also welcoming many of them home. We provide a truly needed respite."

Thompson asked, breaking into their thoughts, "Is it a problem to leave so soon?"

"No, no, no." Alfred waved his free hand like a railroad semaphore. "We can pack up an entire stageset and the costumes and be on the road within a short time after even a late performance." He snapped his fingers. "Just like that."

"We didn't expect to be able to leave so quickly," Lynn added. "But this is a wonderful surprise."

Thompson visibly relaxed a little, shifting to sit up and slide back in the chair. "That's what we were told, that you two could be ready at the drop of a hat. But let me assure you, this is no picnic. The German wolfpacks are still out there, cruising the Atlantic. They seem to be losing steam, but that's no guarantee that you won't be in danger from their U-boats. Since January, we've lost thirteen ships near the Azores, which is right where you're headed."

Lynn and Alfred exchanged looks that spoke of concern and questions.

Thompson continued. "We're sending you on a freighter. There will be a military escort, however, that will join you once you get south of Bermuda. Going south like that should keep you out of the reach of the German U-boats. Your escort will stay within sight and radio contact, just in case. And your freighter will be shadowed by a Brazilian navy vessel."

"A freighter," Alfred said. "Well, that should be interesting."

Thompson gave a short chuckle. "Don't worry. It's fitted out just fine. One of the holds is rebuilt for accommodations. Besides you two, there will be about 125 children and their carers aboard, heading back home to England at the request of their parents, after a three-year separation. They've been housed in Canada up until now."

Lynn thought how terrible it must be for the children separated from their families. And the parents as well. She remembered offering to take the Redgrave children to America for the duration of the war, but Michael and Rachel demurred, citing that the family preferred to remain together, as they couldn't bear to be parted from their children. Plus, the public would expect solidarity from that famous acting family.

But on a ship with 125 children! "How long a voyage, do you know?" Lynn asked the agent.

"Should be not much more than two weeks," Thompson said. "You'll head for the Azores from America, then sail to Lisbon, Portugal. From there, we've made arrangements for a flight to London. We hope that's satisfactory."

Other than flying, which they both abhorred, this was like a dream to Lynn. She and Alfred waited so long to get permission to travel into a war zone. So much paperwork, so many strings to pull, it strained their normally good natures. Now that it seemed all was finally in hand, she shook herself mentally to make sure she was awake, and they would actually be on their way. Details started to pile up in her head. Suitcases, which ones? The steamer trunk, for certain, because they planned on staying in London for the duration of the war, if they could. The costumes and props! They could leave all the details of packing those to the experts at the theater. Lynn revised that thinking. She would stay out of that part, but she knew Alfred would be right in the thick of things. Every detail had to be examined, perhaps revised, checked, double-checked, and finalized before he would be satisfied. She chuckled.

Alfred was talking to her.

"...right, Lynnie?" Alfred asked...something.

"I'm sorry, darling, I was off in a world of my own," she confessed.

"Thinking of everything that must be done, undoubtedly," he said. "Agent Thompson wants to know if we're clear on the paperwork. Is it all in order?"

"Indeed, yes," Lynn said. She sent the agent a glittering smile. "All in order." She leaned over and patted his knee. "We are both delighted that the government will allow us to travel to England."

"How can we deny you?" George said. "You've already done so much work here. The promotion of war bonds, the radio dramas, your work at the Stage Door Canteen, all of it. You helped raise millions of dollars."

Alfred and Lynn shared a look full of satisfaction. "Yes, we do especially love working at the Canteen," Alfred said. He turned to Thompson, as if to share a secret. "Lynn makes the best sandwiches."

"And you are the most glamorous garbageman." Lynn laughed. "Remember the night that soldier called you Alfred Fontanne?"

Alfred chuckled. "Yes, I do. You gave him an extra sandwich."

They settled back into the memory.

Agent Thompson sat up straight and set his arms on the arms of the chair. His relaxed attitude shifted to controlled tension. "That was really valuable work. Now I know you want to bring that valuable work to the besieged folks in England." He cleared his throat.

Lynn was alert to that as a sign Thompson was moving on to something different, something that felt more...ominous? She wasn't sure she was reading the signs correctly. "What is it that you wish to add?" she asked, to draw him out. Her face, she knew, would give nothing away.

"You don't miss a trick, do you, Miss Fontanne?" His tone was serious. "You two are a valuable asset to the war effort. We want to protect you and...enhance all that you bring to England."

Lynn could tell that Alfred caught the miniscule pause. His thigh muscles tensed just a bit under her hand, and she responded with a press of her thumb.

The agent went on before she had a chance to say anything. "We've arranged for someone to meet you in London, just to help you get settled. Since the Blitz, London isn't what it used to be. It never hurts to have a guide in these troublesome times. Consider him your concierge."

This time, Alfred leaned forward and asked, before the agent filled any gap in the conversation. "So, you're really hiring a nanny."

Thompson laughed. "Not hardly, Mr. Lunt. He will be just the thing to help get you settled. We've already made arrangements for you to stay at the Savoy. According to what you told us, that is your preference?"

"Yes, that's our first choice, if the hotel is safe," Alfred said.

"Who is this 'concierge'?" Lynn asked. "And what role exactly is he to play?"

"The man is a wonder at finding things that people need. His name is Hamilton. James Hamilton. You'll probably also meet his wife somewhere along the line. She's a big help with what he does."

Alfred asked, "Tell us a little more about this Hamilton and his wife."

"They're both Irish," Thompson said, then waggled his hand, like a plane's wings. "Well, from the North. So that makes them as much British."

"Which is it?" Lynn asked. "Are they British or Irish?"

"Depends on who you're talking to. But Belfast got blasted by Herr Hitler during the blitz too, so you know whose side they're on, for sure. They work in London now, finding housing where they can for those displaced by the bombing, among other things. So, they get all over the city, and can usually find whatever is needed."

"Does he work for the American State Department?" Alfred probed.

Thompson shook his head. "No, he's employed by the British War Department to help civilians find shelter and food and such."

"You said he has a wife who works with him. What's her name?" Lynn asked. It would be good to have another woman around, in addition to Antoinette. Her poor sister had enough on her plate without being pestered with...who knows what?

"Heather," Thompson answered. "She's been a real boon to James, from what I've heard. She can ferret out food when it seems no one else can." Thompson reached down and rescued his hat from the floor. "If you have any more questions, feel free to call me." He stood, pulled a business card from his inside pocket and handed it to Alfred. He was clearly not going to give them any more information. They were on their own, in spite of that offer.

Alfred rose at the same time, gestured for Thompson to precede him toward the foyer. But the agent was already well on his way.

Lynn waited to hear the muffled goodbyes, the click of the door closing. She gathered their paperwork, slid it all back into the envelope and set it on her lap.

Alfred came back and joined her once again. He crossed his legs, laced his fingers together, and pursed his lips at his wife.

Lynn sighed. He was waiting for her assessment. She launched into her analysis. "There is more going on here than meets the eye, Alfred. But Thompson was not about to share any more with us than he had to. From what I can see, we're going to have to wait until we meet this James Hamilton to glean more information."

"Hamilton may not be very forthcoming either, Lynnie," Alfred said. "But I agree. There's not much more we can wring out of the State Department here."

Lynn patted the packet on her lap. "We have our travel papers. We know when and where we're going. We just need to pack."

"And I say, let's get to it." Alfred stood up and offered her his hand. "I'll call the theater where everything is stored and get things moving."

Lynn tucked the envelope under her arm, grasped Alfred's hand and rose. "I'll pull the suitcases out of storage."

They set off on the start of their newest adventure.

-3-

The pier was uncommonly frantic, or at least it seemed that way to Lynn. Of course, this was a Liberty freighter, not a Cunard liner. The ship, such as she looked down its length, was considerably smaller than she was used to for a transatlantic crossing.

The Liberty ships were built in matter of weeks, rather than the months taken with liners lovingly designed for comfort and luxury. The Liberties had soldered seams rather than the customary–and stronger–riveted joints. Lynn read about one of the Liberty ships breaking cleanly in half shortly after it was launched when the soldering gave way.

These ships, the mules of the sea, carried armaments, tanks, ammunition, foodstuffs and clothing. Compared to their usual mode of travel, the 20th Century Limited train from New York to Chicago, this was bare-bones. No multiroom suites with velvet settees and room service. That much, she knew already. The rest would be revealed as soon as they could board.

She was distracted from her assessments by Alfred's touch on her shoulder.

Alfred promised her an "I won't be long", then left to check on their luggage and, even more important, to confirm that the props crates were on board. The theater where they were stored assured him they were sent down already yesterday, but, Alfred being

Alfred, he needed to see for himself. Heaven forbid if they were not there! He would surely fall into a series of epithets not to be heard in proper company, to be followed soon by a raging headache. Luckily, that didn't happen often, but it had before. Once, after railing at an actor at rehearsal who dared to tease and belittle a fellow actor, Alfred stalked out of the theater to cool off. When he came back, Lynn discovered not only did he have a terrible headache, but he vomited in the interim, so angry he was. Lynn shook her head at the memory of that episode, and hoped it would never be repeated.

As she waited alongside the gangplank, she watched all the comings and goings to keep her mind occupied. The stevedores were swinging trunks and suitcases from trolleys over to men waiting to store them aboard. The rhythm of their work entranced her. Farther down the bulk of the freighter, men were loading provisions, overseen by the cook standing in the opening in the ship's side that probably led to storerooms close to the kitchens. Looking like a conductor, except for his long white apron, he was gesturing, up, down, palm out, hands waving. It was almost a dance. His mouth was wide open and clearly shouting something to his helpers. She was far enough away, lucky, in fact, to be so far away, so as not to hear exactly what he was hollering. She preferred to preserve the belief that it was something musical.

Lynn shifted her attention to the great open warehouse behind her, massive doors wide, gaping as if to swallow the shadow cast by the gargantuan ship, or perhaps the ship itself. Flights of fancy, she thought.

Those flights were disrupted with the cloud of children sweeping her way from the warehouse. Ah, the children heading home to England. Yes, it appeared there were over a hundred of them. Their carers, handlers, escorts, whatever they were called, skittered along the outside like so many border collies herding sheep to the pen. But this flock managed to look a bit more organized, each child carrying one, sometimes two suitcases, the larger children helping the smaller. A few of the women escorts carried toddlers clamped to their bosoms.

Well, Lynn thought, they look quite well-mannered. Perhaps that was more a wish than an accurate assessment, but only time out on the ocean would tell. She tamped down fleeting images of seasickness, children running wild down the decks, the flurry of serving dinner... No, she thought, don't second guess, and don't make an Act Two of it either. Act Two usually contained a climax, and most often, not a pleasant one.

Alfred came along the pier just then, and was caught on the other side of the flow of children, who were now making their way up the gangplank. Lynn watched him watch the children, probably thinking of their own nieces and nephews. It could be a long time before she would be making play dresses out of old newspapers, or teaching one of them how to make trifle, her signature dessert. Truth be told, though she cooked a little, trifle at least was beyond burning or messing up some other way.

The river of children finally was all aboard and Alfred came across to meet her. "All is well, Lynnie. They actually took me on board and showed me the props and costume crates. I spotted your steamer trunk too, so we're all set." He looked around. "Where is our personal luggage? I left it with you on a trolley."

Lynn set her hand on his arm. "Not to worry, darling. I had a porter take it to our stateroom. I watched as he took them up the gangplank, so at least they'll be on the ship somewhere." She knew it was a tease, and hoped it wouldn't honestly worry him.

"Maybe they'll put it all in the captain's suite and we'll have to trade cabins." After his exploration with the theater crates, at least he didn't lose his sense of humor. He offered Lynn his arm and they turned to go up the gangplank.

"Mr. Lunt!" A voice not to be dismissed, it was so deep and loud. And insistent, repetitive. "Mr. Lunt! Wait!" It was coming from the warehouse.

Alfred frowned down at Lynn, a question on his face.

"Don't board yet!"

They finally spotted the man attached to the voice.

He was headed down the pier, directly for them, coattails flapping. He pulled up next to them, puffing like a horse driven to the edge of its speed. "Can't...go." He bent over, hands on knees, to catch his breath.

Lynn shared a sideways glance with Alfred, something between who-is-this-man and I-fear-we're-in-trouble. She wanted to bolt up the gangplank before the sweaty man could begin a tirade of some sort. His red face seemed to preclude a rebuke.

Alfred, for his part, stood relaxed. "Take your time, my good man. But not too much. We've a ship to catch."

At that, the man struggled upright and pulled a wallet out of his coat pocket. He took a deep breath. "You can't go. Mrs. Lunt's application and passport are not legal."

Lynn learned long ago to let the "Mrs. Lunt" go. She was, and always would be "Miss Lynn Fontanne." She held her tongue, anticipating what was coming.

Alfred took over. "Of course they're legal. The man–what was his name again, Lynn?"

"Thompson. Agent George Thompson."

"Yes, that's it." Alfred went on. "Agent Thompson himself delivered our travel papers, including our passports. What's wrong with them?"

"Nothing with yours, Mr. Lunt." The man flashed his State Department badge. But his face was creased with a frown, not a smile. "But with your wife's here. That's the problem."

Alfred took a step back. "Well then, she's the one to talk to, not me." He folded his hands in front of him and waited.

The agent seemed a bit flustered, perhaps not used to dealing with independent women. "Well..." He finally trained his gaze on Lynn. He cleared his throat and shuffled his feet.

"Well?" Lynn rather enjoyed his discomfort. She could easily intuit his concern, but she wasn't about to give an inch. Let him dangle a bit. These men were supposed to be trained and hardened to their roles, but here was an exception.

"Well," the agent repeated, then stopped. Was he going to be only an echo?

Time was running short before embarkation. Lynn took pity. "Show me, please, what is wrong with my papers. I'm sure we can straighten this all out."   She blessed him with one of her understanding smiles.

Finally, he seemed to realize his job. He rescued a paper from an inner pocket, opened it, and pointed to her signature at the bottom. "Right here, Mrs. Lunt."

She ignored the title.

He went on. "See?" He tapped the paper. "You signed it Miss Lynn Fontanne."

"That is correct," she said. "That is my legal name."

"But aren't you married to Mr. Alfred Lunt here?" he asked.

"Yes, of course I am. But my legal name is Fontanne, not Lunt."

He shook his head. "But if you are married, and you are traveling together, then you must travel as Mrs. Lynn Lunt. Anything else makes it illegal in the eyes of State. You should've signed it Lynn Lunt, not Lynn Fontanne."

"You'll have to call Agent Thompson about that," Lynn said. "He didn't seem to have a problem with it. Apparently, neither did the State Department, because that is the name that came on my passport."

The vertical lines between the agent's eyebrows deepened into Grand Canyons. "But–"

He got no further than that one word before Lynn interrupted him with a wave of the hand that was clearly direction to move away. "Go and call. We have a ship to catch, and it won't wait for us. Or for the State Department either." She remembered her good manners. "Please, call your office. We can wait. But don't dawdle, please, we don't have much time." She pointed to the warehouse door. "There is an office just within there. I'm sure they'll let you use their phone. Show them your badge. Government business will take precedence, I'm sure." Then she launched that smile again.

"Don't move," the agent said. He turned away and jogged into the warehouse.

Alfred moved back to take his place next to Lynn. "Charmed another one, Lynnie. Sometimes I don't know how you do it." He lifted her hand and kissed it.

They waited with growing impatience, but finally the agent emerged, waving his hat.

"The way he's acting, it looks like he got the story straight," Alfred said.

As he ran closer, Lynn saw that the frown lines were replaced with a more relaxed face. As he came to a stop in front of them, Lynn said, giving him a chance to catch his breath, "You received your answer, I see. We are free to go?"

"Yes, you are free to go," the agent confirmed. "You should have no more problems."

Perhaps not with State, Lynn thought, but we're going into a war zone. How could we possibly avoid problems? But she fervently hoped they could sidestep any they came across.

"Thank you for checking," Alfred said. "This makes us much more at ease, knowing that everyone is on the same page." He offered his hand, and the agent took it and pumped a vigorous handshake.

With a "bon voyage" and "let us know if we can do anything for you," the agent turned and made his way back into the warehouse.

By this time, the pier was deserted of anyone other than Philadelphia workers.

Lynn grabbed Alfred's arm and steered him to the foot of the gangplank. "Come, Alfred, let's board before the crew berates us as sluggards."

He gave her a grateful glance. She recognized a residue of nervous tension, but knew her touch always calmed him. They headed up. The crew pivoted the gangplank away the moment their feet hit the deck. One sailor slid the railed section across the opening and locked it in place.

The Lunts moved to stand at the rail with the other passengers, a goodly way down from all the children, and waved at the stevedores as the great ship eased away from the pier.

~4~

The first look at their stateroom sent Lynn into gales of laughter, which she valiantly tried to stifle. "A senior officer gave up his quarters for us so we could have a private bathroom. Even at that, it's not very spacious, is it? I think we've retrogressed to our honeymoon days."

"Looks like it." He chuckled. "That bunk is no bigger than our first bed in the townhouse."

"Well, it was a generous offer, and we can graciously accept." It would do. It would have to.

As they stepped into the cabin, Lynn noted the tiny bathroom to their left, paired with an equally small closet to their right. On the same wall as the door was a very small desk bolted to the floor, with shelves stacked above, and a chair below. A built-in bench took up the remainder of the space along the wall. The bunk was squeezed in along the far bulkhead under a small porthole. Not much room for a six-foot two-inch Alfred, much less the pair of them.

"Bloomingdales must have sent the ship a three-quarter bed, just like they did for us, even though we ordered a double." Lynn's eyes sparkled with the memory of them spooning, legs tucked up and Alfred's arms wrapped around her.

"Well, we managed before, we can do it again," Alfred said. "That was what? Twenty-one years ago."

"Happy anniversary, darling. Here we are again." She tossed her coat onto the bunk. "Only this time, I think we should share. One night, I'll squash up against the bulkhead, and then we can switch the next night."

"God forbid the inside person has to get up during the night," Alfred's face was a study in serious concern.

But Lynn could read him like a book. "Don't worry dear, I'll only step on your legs if I have to get up. It would be a shame to damage that handsome puss of yours." She turned to plant a kiss on Alfred's nose.

The first days on the water promised clear sailing, although the seas were rather choppy. Nothing unusual, apparently. The weather was partly sunny, with what looked like benign clouds scudding across the sky. Lynn enjoyed taking the sun in a deck chair, while Alfred strode the decks, talking with crew members and guests alike.

The children were surprisingly jolly and obedient. The journey was much more of a lark for them, going home to families in England. They cruised the decks, teasing each other and bumping against walls before they got their sea legs. Their laughter was a sharp contrast to the thoughts of the London warzone surely occupying the minds of the adults. Yet, the children helped everyone relax a degree or two.

That happy picture changed rapidly.

Nearing Bermuda, the skies began frowning, clouds building up into towers, winds eventually reaching cyclonic proportions. Lynn stayed indoors and Alfred took to pacing the corridors before settling like a peripatetic bird next to Lynn in what passed as the salon on the freighter. Bare tables and chairs, and not much more. The carers had installed boxes of toys and games for their charges, which gave it more the feel of a nursery, rather than a salon for adults looking for somewhere to perch, other than their staterooms. No overstuffed chairs, no drapery, no waiter hovering ready to take drink orders. Lynn didn't mind. They didn't sign up for comfort, after all. She thought of the boys struggling against all odds across the mined fields and roadways of France and beyond. She was quite well satisfied to be somewhere where she wasn't being bombed. In spite of the U-boat.

The children were confined to the salon as well, though their numbers dropped dramatically by the hour as a few at a time succumbed to seasickness. Many of them retreated to their bunks in the refitted hold. Lynn inquired, and was told that, in addition to cots, hammocks were hung to provide more sleeping berths. She pictured them swinging wildly, and had to hang onto her stomach and purge her mind to keep nausea at bay. Incessantly, the seas slammed against the ship and the wind howled. Old King Neptune seemed determined to punish them for invading his kingdom.

"I'm going to the stateroom, Alfred," Lynn said. "I'm not feeling well at all." She took herself off in haste, hoping to reach the bathroom before her stomach gave up its contents.

Alfred, whose stomach up to this point was always a bit tetchy, as his mother put it years before, looked just a tad green along the gills, nothing worse. He waved off Lynn. "I'm going to hold down the fort here for a while. I want to get out on deck. The fresh air will revive me."

Lynn didn't take the time to answer, but she was sure the crew wouldn't let him out in this kind of weather. She could just picture him blown overboard. But she didn't dare slow down or stop to warn him. Leave it to the experts, she thought, and headed below.

Alfred joined her an hour or so later. Was it only an hour? she thought. It felt like an eternity. She spent some time cradling her best friend, the toilet bowl, before she had nothing left to offer, not even a dry retch. She retired to their bunk and tried to ignore the pitching and rolling. She did get a little comfort from being horizontal. But little was the operative word.

When Alfred appeared, he carried a thermos and a plate of something she hoped she wouldn't have to eat. But when he uncorked the thermos, the most wonderful aroma of Earl Grey tea wafted over to her. She propped herself up on one elbow. "Yes, please. I'll take some of that."

Alfred chuckled. "I haven't even offered it yet." He set out two cups and saucers on their little table, wedging the pot in its cozy up against the brass rail that surrounded the edge. "The cook says not to add milk or sugar. It'll just upset your stomach more."

Lynn nearly retched at the thought of milk or sugar, but managed to keep her composure. "Perfect. Please, Alfred, a cuppa." She propped herself up against a stack of pillows and was ready when Alfred delivered a cup half full of tea. One sip and she felt the restorative warmth cascade down to her stomach. She waited, hoping. No, this was the perfect remedy. It stayed down.

They spent the next three days in their cabin, not daring to venture out. They wondered how the children were faring. The decks outdoors were off limits now, which meant the hold where the children slept and the salon, where everyone ate in shifts, were certainly crowded. Earlier, Lynn watched the carers corralling and shepherding their charges, keeping the little ones busy, making space and time for naps, doing all they could. Lynn wasn't up to helping just yet, but maybe once the storm abated. She and Alfred were good at entertaining nieces and nephews... But right now, they could still hear the storm pounding and raging. Not much was visible out the porthole. Angry waves, water. Water and more water. The sky was visible only when the ship rolled, and then it was hard to tell the gray water from the even grayer sky.

"Are we going in circles, Alfred?" Lynn asked the second day of the storm.

"I'm going up to check. It feels to me too that we're not making any headway." He came over and kissed the top of her head. "I'll be back soon."

"Be careful, darling," she said. "I'd hate to lose you to Davy Jones's Locker. "I'd come with you, but–"

"Don't even think about it, Lynnie. You're better off prone. That seems to be keeping you in check." He slipped out the door and was gone.

Lynn lay back on her bank of pillows and closed her eyes. The storm took away her ability to sleep deeply through anything. But at least she wasn't getting sick anymore. The big liners they usually travelled on encountered weather, surely, but nothing like this. Plus, this was a freighter, not built for pleasure cruises. One would think they were better able to handle high seas, considering their bulk. But perhaps even the Cunard liners, the queens of the seas, would roll and yaw. The brute seas could probably cudgel anything, the way it felt.

She fell asleep, but when Alfred returned–how long was he gone? She had no idea. The rattle of the door handle had her awake in an instant. She turned her head and smiled at him, but opted not to raise her head and bring on any demons that might be lying in wait. "What did you find out?"

"We're right. They're going in circles. The captain is trying to maneuver around what has turned into a full-blown hurricane." He made his way to the little bench, luckily bolted to the wall, holding onto anything that offered a firm purchase. He dropped down like a thrown sack of potatoes.

Lynn blanched. "Can he do that? It feels like we're trapped."

"According to him–well, really, his staff. He's far too busy to talk to me. And they wouldn't let me up on the bridge. Anyway, all the weather signs point to it moving itself off sometime tomorrow. I was told just to stay in my cabin and ride it out. The ship is doing fine." He shifted around until he was settled. "One more day, Lynnie. We can hold out that long."

Lynn sighed. "It's a good thing we're not heading for an opening night. At least, we have some wiggle room in our calendar. Lisbon, here we come...I hope."

That roused Alfred, who was working to stretch out a bit more, levering off his shoes and setting his feet on the bunk. "First the Azores, I was told. Then Lisbon."

"Why the Azores, I wonder?" Lynn said.

"Something about taking on troops to get them on to Lisbon. Where they go beyond that, I have no idea. I wouldn't ask anyway. Loose lips sink ships. Isn't that the way it goes?"

Lynn nodded. "We're a full ship already, packed in cheek by jowl, to say nothing of the goods in the holds. I wonder where they'll put all the soldiers?" No answer from Alfred. Sure enough, he was settled in place, his hands clutching the rail running along the sides of the bench, apparently asleep. First a hurricane, she thought. I wonder what's next. The immediate thought was of the wolf packs of U-boats harassing ships crossing the Atlantic. Most of those seemed to be operating north of where they were crossing, which is why they were crossing so far south. Her mind drifted to the Brazilian navy ship that would meet and follow them, once this storm abated. If all went well...

She slipped into sleep before her mind could take her into even more dangerous waters.

~5~

By the time the *Stage Door Canteen* was mid-Atlantic, having ridden out the hurricane with minimum damage, most of it to their psyches, the passengers settled into a routine that didn't have much variety. The seas settled into comforting rolls, placid rather than displaying Neptune's anger. Sunny days invited passengers to recline in a deck chair, preferably with a ship's throw to encase the legs, with a good book. Or for Lynn and Alfred, a script. Even if the freighter didn't have all the amenities of their usual ocean liners, it did have a shuffle board area and a small library. Even working sailors needed something to do on their rare down time. And watching the children provided its own kind of entertainment.

If it were cloudy, or the sea was somewhat unsettled, then the salon worked fine, though it was a bit tight, what with children playing board games, or begging one of their carers to read them a story.

After observing long stretches of boredom in the children, and listening to their complaints, Lynn convinced Alfred to help her put together a skit to involve the children and pass the time.

Now, after satisfactorily busy days of collaborative writing and then rehearsing, the Lunts were back in their stateroom, having pulled off a command evening performance by the children. The night was still young for most theater people, but this time, they were tired, and changed into nightclothes the moment they were alone. The only concession to the cool temperatures was to leave their socks on. They took time to re-hash their efforts.

"That boy...how old was he, Alfred? Do you know?" Lynn said. "He was terrific as the Beast at Sea."

"Twelve, I think," Alfred said. "He was quite good, wasn't he? Stomping around and growling."

"How delightful that the cook just jumped right in to help with costumes."

"Who would think to use a colander for a crown?" Alfred laughed.

"You would! Are you sure you didn't help out with that idea?" When Alfred shook his head, Lynn went on. "Even better, the cook wired forks, tines up, all around the outside to make it look like a crown."

"Personally, I was sorely tempted to steal the Beast's trident. Even though I've got plenty at home, that meat fork had me salivating. It was a beauty."

Lynn chuckled. "And how would you get it off the broom handle quickly enough to abscond with it? We'd never get it past the authorities in Lisbon either. They'd be convinced you went daft, bringing such a 'medieval weapon' into the war." She sat down and patted the bunk beside her in an invitation, which Alfred accepted.

"I liked the little girl who played Beauty," Alfred said. "She looked like such a waif in the chef's white coat. Even though a lot of the children opted out of being in the performance, they did make an appreciative audience. We did quite a good job of including all the children that did want in, if I say so myself. They made such cute little mermaids and mermen, blowing bubbles from the cook's soap solution."

"My absolute favorite," Lynn said, "was that one little tyke at the very end, when the Beast and Beauty crushed the real Beast of the Ocean, and–"

"The two went off to live happily ever after," Alfred finished.

"No, that's not my favorite part. The best part was right after that, when that tiny little girl in the audience called out, 'Now they killed all the Germans and we can go home!'" Lynn leaned into Alfred's shoulder, and they both sat silent. Their ocean voyage would end, and they–children as well–would be thrust into a world where all the Germans had not been killed. Yet, Lynn hoped.

She shook herself, sat up straight, and set off on a brighter tack. "We weren't such strict taskmasters as we are with ourselves, Alfred, but we certainly put together a smash hit anyway." Lynn lifted her arms to the ceiling. "Beauty and the Seabeast Afloat! A triumph!"

"Next stop, Broadway." Alfred laughed. "I honestly don't know how you do it, darling. Too bad we didn't have any old newspapers so you could make paper dresses and whatnot for more costumes."

"Well, we made do quite well, didn't we? With a lot of help from everyone." Lynn sighed. "We ourselves played any number of times without costumes when we were on tour. Sometimes the props and costume trunks just didn't get to us on time."

"I always offered to refund the ticket price, if people were unhappy."

"You knew perfectly well no one would ask," Lynn said.

"I didn't know it the first time we tried it," Alfred said. "I was a nervous Nellie." He blew her a kiss.

Lynn dropped off her slippers and pulled her feet up under her. "I think our reputations are intact." She leaned back against the bulkhead. It was a lot of work and time to put together even that little skit, but it was worth it. The children loved it. "Such fun when they called us the Fabulous Lunts."

"I like Laurence Olivier's nickname for us. The Celestials." Alfred swiveled to lie down and set his stocking feet in her lap. "Hope you don't mind," he said, pointing at his toes.

Lynn shook her head. "You're just too tall to stretch out, Alfred. But I wouldn't have you any other way."

"I am exhausted," Alfred said. "I vote for a good night's sleep and a hearty breakfast in the morning."

"I second that motion." Lynn slid along the bulkhead until she could lay her head on Alfred's shoulder. She rolled so her back was against the bulkhead. "Just pull the blanket up, would you, darling?"

Alfred wriggled up against her. "Spooning works best." He grabbed the blanket on the foot of the bed and flung it across the two of them. "I'm too tired to even brush my teeth."

"As long as you're facing away, I won't complain." Lynn raised herself up enough to give him a kiss on the ear. The mumble he returned assured her he must be halfway to dreaming already.

* * *

The blaring of the klaxon raised Lynn upright and crouched on the bunk before she came fully awake. Alfred was already standing, having flung out of bed before she had a chance to react. The ship was rolling and pitching. She heard rhythmic drumming, the ferocious onslaught like a thunder god rearing back, then slamming waves against the hull. "What–"

Alfred was already swinging into action. "Come on, Lynnie!" He stepped awkwardly into his trousers. "This doesn't feel like a drill! Quick! Clothes! We've got to get up on deck!"

Lynn was up and pulling a sweater over her head without bothering to take off her nightgown. She pulled on a pair of pants and stuffed the length of the nightgown into the waistband as best she could, then rammed her feet into shoes. It didn't pay to try and talk to Alfred. The sound of the boat drill horn blasted away any hope of communication. They both swayed as the boat rocked, fighting to maintain equilibrium.

Alfred was tying his shoes as she managed to get on her coat. She grabbed their passports and jammed them into the pocket, then dropped to her knees to drag out their lifejackets from under the bunk.

Alfred was at the door, waving her on with frantic gestures. She could see his mouth forming, "Come on! Come on!", though she could barely hear him over the siren.

They joined the stream of people making their way along the corridor. The younger children were housed in the crew quarters, while the crew members slung hammocks in the hold reconfigured with bunks for the older children, so the younger ones here were like a herd of newborn sheep, ricocheting to and fro off the walls, as well as being pulled and encouraged along by the carers.

The corridor was getting crowded with crying children, and carers trying their best to hurry them along. A bottleneck formed as one of the carers, herding several small children and carrying two more young ones, was caught in a whirlpool of children swirling around her. More and more children were caught up in the maelstrom. It seemed a futile effort for her to unravel.

Alfred, coming up behind, slid in between where he could, and scooped up a child under each arm. Lynn took one baby from the carer. The jam loosened and, led by Alfred creating a looser wake, everyone was able to move forward. They headed up and out to the deck. The organized chaos there showed, with the staff shunting people to their lifeboat stations as fast as they could.

The morning was barely awake, with the tip of the sun ready to plunge into the clouds gathered at the horizon. Everything was rather leaden. Water, sky, small tendrils of fog. With the rolling of the ship, it was hard to see anything clearly. In the somber dawn, color was washed out of the ship, the faces, the clothing. Even the khaki lifejackets were faded to a pale shade.

Lynn and Alfred wound their way around and through, until they reached their particular children's designated gathering spot. They deposited their burdens and moved along to their own station. They huddled with a clutch of other passengers, everyone talking at once, until they were warned to keep silent.

Suddenly, their escort destroyer appeared off their port flank, zigzagging at high speed, heading out and away from the *Canteen*.

"Look!" Alfred said, one arm around Lynn and the other pointed out to sea. "A periscope, I think!"

As the destroyer moved out, they caught glimpses of a metallic finger rising out of the sea. "Periscope," one of the crew confirmed.

Crew members strode across the front of the crowds, frowning, fingers on lips, one arm pointing out to sea. What looked like a gray whale was breaching, its back barely visible between distant swells. A German U-boat. It had to be. Heading toward where they were gathered.

Silence reigned, except for the whimpering of the youngest children.

The escort ship sped out, guns firing erratically whenever the sub showed itself.

The destroyer, like a drone protecting the queen bee, was out there, between the lumbering Liberty ship with its 125 children and the U-boat. It was terrible to be unable to see what was happening, until the escort faded back a bit. Unsettling to think that the *Canteen* would probably be unable to get the kind of speed to outrun any German submarine. Lynn had no idea how fast a German submarine could move. That didn't help.

Alfred leaned down to whisper in Lynn's ear. "I think they might have to surface to shoot at us."

She didn't know if that was true either. Her heart was pounding, and she could feel Alfred's match hers, as she huddled against him.

Lynn sent up a fervent prayer that the U-boat would sink beneath the waves and leave them. The *Canteen* had a big gun at the bow and another at the stern, but that wasn't much against a German sub. The Liberty ships relied on their escorts, which carried depth charges. But that meant...what? Getting close enough? Getting over the U-boat? Lynn didn't know. Another level of anxiety.

She wanted to squeeze her eyes shut, but couldn't tear her gaze away from the drama developing in front of them. The U-boat was clearer now, cutting along through the water. Still far enough off, Lynn hoped. She thought of the nickname Wolf Pack given to the prowling U-boats. This one looked to be a lone wolf, however. No other wakes or gray tubes, just the one.

The seas were getting restless, the waves rolling and growing. The troughs deepened as the crests heightened. Time seemed to slow to a crawl. Which was the top speed of their ship as well. A crawl. Too slow.

The U-boat was no longer visible as it neared and suddenly sank below the surface.

The escort swung to confront the threat.

The *Canteen*, facing into the waves, began plunging, her flank exposed to the escort and the sub who were dancing a lethal two-step. Bow up, stern down. Bow down, stern up. Again. And again.

Lynn found her hands clenched tight in the depths of her coat pockets. So tight that her nails bit into her palms. She couldn't loosen them.

As Lynn watched, two long wakes shot out from under the sea. From the U-boat, without a doubt. Torpedoes. Her hands went without direction to tighten the straps on her lifejacket before reaching out to secure Alfred's hand in a vise grip. She took in a great breath and held it.

At that moment, they plunged over the crest of a wave, bringing the stern up to the sky.

The two foaming wakes disappeared under the lifted stern of the *Canteen*. Lynn heard cheers from the starboard side of their boat. Passengers and crew cheering. The cry went up and down the line. "The torpedoes passed right under us!" "The stern was so high, nothing hit!"

A miracle.

Several geysers erupted from beyond their escort ship. Right on the heels of those, momentous booms reached their ears. "Depth charges!" Alfred hollered. "From the escort!"

Within a few moments, there was no long gray whale. No U-boot visible. No periscope. Nothing.

"Did we get 'em?" rang up and down the deck. No one was sure. Silence.

Everyone watched the escort ship prowl farther out, then swing back.

No sign of trouble.

The all-clear siren finally blew and the atmosphere among the passengers tangibly lifted. The captain came on the loudspeaker and assured them that the threat was over. The U-boat disappeared under the waves, and no sign of it remained.

"I'll bet it turned tail and ran," Alfred said. "They probably shot off their last two torpedoes and then hotfooted it out of there."

The adults around them nodded. "Hope they're gone for good then," one man said.

"Don't even think otherwise," Lynn said, her voice quiet, "or we'll be a bag of nerves the rest of the voyage. Think of the children."

That stifled concerns, at least voiced ones. The crew helped children remove lifejackets, and shepherded everyone along the deck and back to cabins and into the salon.

With the crowds thinned, Lynn turned to Alfred. "I guess nobody told the Germans they were supposed to stay up north farther." She blew out a large breath of gratitude. "I need a cup of tea. I don't even care that we're not dressed as we should be, let's get breakfast."

"Your wish is my command, ma'am." Alfred offered his arm to Lynn. They set off to restore order to their morning.

~6~

The remaining days until they reached the Azores were uneventful, though more people milled around on deck than previously. Some of the children even insisted on wearing their lifejackets for a day or two longer. The mood went from "Isn't the weather just delightful this morning?" to "Have you seen any 'gray whales' this morning?". Their luck held, and no more U-boats appeared. Nor did any other traffic.

They began seeing planes, which terrified them, until the captain assured them that those were British planes going out from the Azores to provide air protection for the Liberty convoys crossing the Atlantic farther north, those delivering food, clothing, military equipment to the barricaded British, who could get nothing from the continent anymore.

In a fortuitous move, just the month before, neutral Portugal signed an agreement to allow Allied airfields to be built in the Azores.

"Churchill had a hand in this, I'd bet," Alfred said at dinner one night.

"We heard he invoked an old–and I mean *really* old– treaty between the Brits and the Portuguese," another man at the table offered.

"Wouldn't put it past him," a third said. "He's a wily one, that one."

The captain, when pressed to offer his insights, merely smiled and kept eating.

Dinner and deck conversations swirled around the war. Troop movements were obscured in secrecy, of course, but that still left plenty to chew on. Rumors, and more than just rumors, of concentration camps, killing camps. Those discussions were relegated to the deck, not the dinner table.

Once the planes were spotted, the rails were crowded with passengers searching the horizon for sign of land. Before long, the Azores came into view.

When the *Canteen* docked, Lynn joined the others to watch soldiers unload armaments, crates of ammunition, foodstuffs, and many other boxes holding unnamed cargo. So much that Lynn stopped a crewman to get more details.

"Yes, ma'am. One hold was designated for these folks here, the military," he said, "once we got the crates unloaded."

"One hold?" she asked. Lynn knew that one hold had been refitted with bunks and such for the children and their carers. Were there more than two?

"Yes, ma'am. We've got five holds," the sailor said. "With one empty now, we've got room for the troops." He pointed to the warehouse at the dockside. "See there? About ready to embark."

Lynn squinted in the fall sunlight and peered into the warehouse. What she took as workers became soldiers, duffels at their feet, helmets and other equipment clustered with them. They were too far away to see if they were seasoned troops or very young men. Though most all troops were veterans of campaigns by this time in the war. "Oh my! They're coming on board? Going to Lisbon with us as well? Where do they go from there?" She wondered how many of her questions would get answered.

"Lisbon, yeah. No idea where they'll be deployed from there." The sailor took a step back. "Gotta get back to work." He smiled.

"Pretty safe travel with 200 soldiers on board." He spun and jogged away down the deck.

Alfred joined her. "More company. Makes me sick to think about those young men going into the jaws of–"

"Don't say it, Alfred," Lynn said, laying her hand on his arm. "Don't even think it."

The soldiers moved in a neat phalanx and marched into the hold, empty now of its cargo. Two hundred bodies. Food for cannons and tanks. Lynn was horrified at the thoughts risen unbidden. "Our play is so important. I see that even more now," Lynn said. "It's a tough one, but it shows the backbone needed to withstand the crisis."

"A pacifist family finally coming to terms with their love of country, and how they need to defend it," Alfred said. "A worthy message." He lifted his shoulders and blew out a deep breath. "Come on, Lynnie. Let's get our scripts and see what else we can polish."

* * *

On the afternoon of the third day out from the Azores, the *Stage Door Canteen* pulled up and tied off at the Lisbon quay. The news from the north Atlantic was heartening, as the wolf packs of U-boats diminished considerably. The scuttlebutt was that the Germans lost too many ships and submarines to sustain war at sea. It seemed true, as fewer Allied ships were attacked as the late summer wore on and the fall approached.

The troops evaporated into Lisbon, perhaps bound for war in Italy, considering the Allies established a foothold there barely two months before, and would need reinforcements. On the other hand, the children were bundled off to the airport to be airlifted to London. The Lunts joined the children in a hangar while they waited to board the plane.

"I'm really not looking forward to this, Lynnie," Alfred said, as he did every time he had to fly.

"I know, I know. Neither am I," Lynn agreed. "I am terrified of flying, and if you weren't with me, I might just opt to walk."

Alfred gathered her into a hug. "You might get over the mountains, but you certainly wouldn't get across France. There's no Free France anymore. The Jerries took over everything."

Lynn shivered. "I think I'll be fine once I'm with Antoinette in London. Well, as fine as I can be. You know, she wrote that the house where I posed for the de Glehns was destroyed in the blitzes. I have fond memories of their green front door. The entry into another world."

"I hope they were able to save the supplies from their studio," Alfred said. "And the paintings you modeled for."

Lynn knew there wasn't much chance of that, not from the descriptions her sister sent. She could barely wait to see Tony, and wondered how much of the placid determination shown in her letters from London was only a front. How could anyone live in a city where so much was gone? Running into the Underground at the air raid siren. Spending the night, hoping the rubble wouldn't trap you under there. Creeping up once the all-clear sounded to find...what? Nothing where there had been something? She couldn't bear to think of it.

And yet, given a few more hours, she and Alfred would be in the thick of it.

~7~

When they landed in London, Alfred had a blistering earache. Lynn could breathe, but she felt like jello inside. Flying petrified her, but she felt even worse for poor Alfred with his painful stuffed sinuses and his earache.

They stepped off onto the tarmac. "I almost want to kneel down and kiss the ground," Lynn said. "I can't believe we're actually back. I'm home again. I can't wait to see Antoinette."

A man in a dark coat and hat, nothing military, stepped forward to greet them, flashing an officially embossed badge that identified him as James Hamilton, the man they were told would meet them. He was rather slight with a ruddy complexion and a ready smile. His deep-set eyes gleamed as he swept off his hat in greeting. "I'm James Hamilton, your liaison," he said, confirming their belief. He put his hat back on and took Lynn's makeup kit from her. "I'm here to get you safely settled at the Savoy, and in London in general."

"Is my sister waiting at the hotel? I really am excited to see her again."

"She will meet us there soon. In fact, she may be there already."

"Delightful!" Lynn said. "Lead away."

Alfred took a different tack, clearly anxious to get to the hotel and hopefully rid himself of his pain. "We were told you would meet us at some point. Didn't tell us when, though."

"I'm pleasantly surprised it's this soon," Lynn said. "London must look a lot different than when we were here just a few short years ago."

"Very," Hamilton said, his mouth a wry smile. "But let's get your luggage stowed and get you to the hotel. You'll get an eyeful on the way." He led them toward an official looking military car. "How was the flight?"

Alfred groaned. "All I want is a bed and a soft pillow to lay my head on. I have the most atrocious earache. Happens too often with planes."

Hamilton shook his head. "I can imagine. Same thing happens with me on boats. Crossing the Channel is nigh on impossible." He gave a half-laugh. "Of course, that is truly impossible now anyway, unless you're a soldier heading for the front." He handed them into the back seat of the car.

Lynn stepped in and Alfred flopped beside her. He slid down so he could rest his head back. He closed his eyes. But his good manners came to the fore. "Thank you for meeting us, Mr. Hamilton. I don't think I could manage this. And our–" It was the beginning of a question.

"Call me James," Hamilton said, before closing the back door. "You'll be seeing a fair amount of me, now and again."

Lynn took up Alfred's question. "And our luggage? All of it?"

The driver turned in his seat. "Oh, don't worry about your luggage, sir. It will appear in your suite within a short time."

"And our costumes?" Lynn asked. "The props? What about those?"

James Hamilton got in the front seat, closed the door and swiveled so he could talk to them. "Arrangements all made. They'll go to the theater in Liverpool, as you directed."

Lynn breathed a sigh of relief and reached out to squeeze Alfred's hand. She was rewarded by a small smile. "Lovely. We open in Liverpool, then go on to a few other counties before we take it to London."

"But," Alfred said, "we need a few days at the Savoy to recover."

"That's why I'm here," James said. "To get you settled. You'll be under the aegis of the American USO Camp Shows, designated as captains. They help us keep track of performers and where they can best be used to entertain. You'll be doing shows for the boys, I understand."

"Whatever and wherever we can help," Lynn said.

"You'll be part of the usual circuit," James said, "but not restricted to just that. We know you want to do shows for the citizens, as well as the military. So, in London, you'll be based at the Aldwych Theatre."

"Perfect." Alfred's voice sounded stronger, and he levered himself up to sit up enough to see out the windows. "Now, show us London. We heard about the Blitz from Lynn's sister, but..."

"You want to see it for yourself," James filled in.

Lynn said, "We want to help wherever we can, not just in the theater. If there are volunteer opportunities where we can be useful, please use us."

"Don't worry. There are plenty of places to help. With so many boys on the Continent, we can use you. More on that later. I'm a liaison with all the various groups for you. I'll get you information."

"I understand you're a real theater aficionado, James," Lynn said.

"Yes," he confirmed. "My wife too. You'll like her. She works with the ARP."

"The ARP?" Alfred asked. "What's that?"

"That's the Air Raid Precautions. They help people at bombed out sites, among other things. That's part of what I do too." He swung around to face forward. "We're getting closer."

The outskirts of the city gradually flanked the road as they moved along.

Lynn was eager to see her home country, her beloved London, and her sister. Although, from what she heard through Antoinette's letters, the city would be unrecognizable. The Blitz of the previous three years, to say nothing of the near continual bombing now, would certainly have taken its toll. Lynn braced herself.

But she was not prepared for what she saw. Not at all.

As they drove, the destruction appalled her. Once it started, there was nothing gradual about it. Country gave way immediately to destruction. Piles of rubble, reaching up to the second floors. Broken pavement, forcing the driver to detour around potholes big enough to swallow the car.

Some buildings were without front walls, as if a giant built a dollhouse for the children. Bathtubs and toilets hung by their plumbing, no floors supporting them. Kitchens seemed ready for the cook, if only the gas lines weren't twisted and braided, cut off from their fuel supply.

In several buildings, the top floors were totally gone, but people still clung to the lower floors, unsafe as they appeared. Children clambered over the piles of rubble, searching for...Lynn couldn't imagine anything could have survived such destruction. But as they were forced into slow progress, she watched one little girl retrieve a doll from under a brick. She brandished it in triumph. A moment of joy in the midst of such sorrow.

One street looked untouched, until Lynn craned her neck around to peer down a side street. Every building had an intact front wall, with nothing, nothing at all, behind it. The only indication of damage was the rows of windows with the glass blasted out. Some of those, she found strangely beautiful, as if they stood in defiance of the nightly bombs.

Finally, she leaned against Alfred and closed her eyes. "I can't stand it, Alfred. So hideous, so inhumane."

The car eventually slowed and came to a stop. When she opened her eyes, Lynn saw her beloved Savoy Hotel with its familiar pair of revolving doors.

-8-

The Savoy was looking rather worn, but mostly untouched, in spite of Antoinette's account of bomb damage from the Blitz, when a bomb hit the roof and one of the rooms, killing two people along the way. The hotel, defiant as ever, never closed. However, gone were the days of wild parties and disregard of, or at least turning a blind eye to, the threat looming on the continent. The bombing took care of that. The hotel was still a base for important people, Churchill included, according to many accounts. Still a central gathering place for the wealthy and high-born. Perhaps it was because the hotel was reputed to have the most luxurious, if that was the correct word, air raid shelter in the city. Nothing but the best for the patrons of the Savoy. But above all, the serious side of life became the norm.

None of the dangers or threats swayed the Lunts for long. Their choice was to come to London, no matter the conditions. Lynn hoped for a safe place, a relatively comfortable place, an island of surety and shelter in a world of upheaval. Perhaps the Savoy could retain that aspect for them. It always had before.

But after seeing the war-torn streets of London, Lynn suspended any expectations. She would take it all one day at a time and hope they could bring a message of hope, and an urge to remain steadfast, to the citizens. She was not about to give up.

As bellboys moved to load their luggage onto a cart and take it into the hotel, Alfred handed Lynn out of the car. They made their goodbyes to James, who promised to get in touch once they returned to London. He assured them he was but a phone call away, should they need him before they set out on tour. He clambered back into the car and was gone in a trice.

The Lunts entered the lobby. Lynn didn't expect the customary urns of flowers, or the sense of ease and composure from previous visits, but she wasn't quite prepared for the sandbags adorning the floor below the windows and piled hither and yon, seemingly without purpose. But Lynn knew better than to consider them useless. If nothing else, they did lend an air of care and security.

They moved toward the reception desk, making their way through the bustling traffic of top-brass military men with combat boots below and gleaming stars on their lapels, as well as well-heeled civilians, women draped in fur collars and men in dinner jackets. Sometimes, the more things changed, the more they stayed the same.

As she gazed around the lobby, she spotted the familiar small table near the reception desk, and smiled. *Ah, you're still here.* The large statue of a black cat seemed to send her a sideways glance that said, "Where did you expect I would be?" She strolled over and patted it on the head. "Dear Kaspar, it looks like you'll not have to be the fourteenth guest at dinner anytime soon. I can't imagine there are large dinner parties of thirteen now, what with rationing and all." The cat, long tail curled up and around, merely maintained its silent, slightly aloof, demeanor. "You may have to forage the mouse dens for your dinner now, my pet." She knew the staff would never allow such a degrading activity for their famous mascot sculpture. With a laugh and a final caress of the sculpture, Lynn joined Alfred at the reception desk.

Alfred signed the guest register and the clerk handed the keys to their suite to a bellboy, and gave a letter to Lynn.

"Sorry we can't give you anything bigger, sir," the clerk said. "The military bigwigs need some of the rooms, and the folks who had to evacuate their damaged homes filled the rest, so we've put you in the best two-room suite available. The bathroom is en suite, of course."

"I just have one question," Alfred said.

Lynn tuned out, knowing Alfred was undoubtedly asking about "borrowing" the hotel kitchen so he could do some of his own cooking. She pulled out the note the clerk handed her and scanned for the signature at the bottom. Antoinette. Yes! As she read, her lower lip formed a pout. When she heard Alfred say something about "a shame," she was pulled back to the hotel lobby.

"We can get you a hot plate," the clerk was saying. "But you'll have to keep it in the bathroom. Fire precautions, you know."

Sure enough, Alfred asked about cooking accommodations. He always did. It was one of the things that calmed his nerves. Few things outside the theater pleased him more than being lavishly complimented on his roasted vegetables. She doubted there would be much in the line of variety here, considering.

Alfred was used to occasional cooking, even when staying in a hotel on tour. Somehow, he'd finagle access to the kitchen for himself and their Wisconsin cook, who often traveled with them. The two would create something special for their closest friends. Eggs from their own chickens were toted all over the country, and Ben, their caretaker, would send parcels full of butter and produce, sometimes even preserved meat. Ten Chimneys' bounty was never far away.

But here, at the Savoy, without their cook, who was denied a visa because of war restrictions, and few packages from home, to say nothing of a war on, Alfred would most likely be denied entry to the hotel kitchens. Well, they faced worse while on tour. It would have to do.

When Alfred turned from the reception desk, she got the chance to voice her frustration. "Oh, Alfred! Tony can't meet us. She's finally been accepted into the Women's Land Army. She writes she'll be settling Land Girls at various farms to help where men were conscripted into the army. All those farms that lost workers to the military can get Land Girls to come out and take up the slack until the war is over. Also, she'll be out canvassing the counties, and evaluating lands that can be reclaimed for agriculture. Which means we won't see her for a good long while. I'm so disappointed." She took one last look at Antoinette's note, then took care to fold it and return it to its envelope before depositing the note in her purse.

"So sorry about Tony. We'll try to connect as soon as we can. She'll do a crackerjack job for the Land Army, I'm sure." Alfred tucked her hand into the crook of his elbow. "Shall we go up, Lynnie? Unfortunately, it's not possible for me to use the kitchen, but they will provide a hot plate, as long as I promise to use it only in the bathroom."

"I heard." Lynn smiled at the image of Alfred whipping up liver and onions in the bathroom. She stifled that when she saw his expression. He didn't look completely desolate, but Lynn could feel his pain. "Your meals are delicious anyway, dear," she said. "And what you don't whip up here, we can get in the dining room downstairs."

"Pretty plain stuff, Lynnie," Alfred said.

They headed for the lifts, following their bellboy.

"You can't complain too much. I heard that the Savoy keeps its own flock of chickens. It's a way to ensure they can get fresh eggs and meat."

"I know, I know. But I miss my cream and sugar. Rationing is really cutting down on what we can get. And how much." He seemed to catch himself. "But I'm really not complaining. Look at how London has pulled itself together. I can't imagine."

"We're doing fine," Lynn said. "You're right. The people here are so brave. They never give up. I really don't hear too much about them complaining, though they certainly have earned the right."

"The English stiff upper lip and all," Alfred said. "There's a lot to be said for that. Old Mr. Hitler didn't know what he was taking on when he set his sights on this island."

"I'm anxious to begin acting. I think people are going to be able to let down their hair a bit. They'll see themselves in the play's family that is holding out against the enemy. Maybe it will act as a bit of a catharsis," Lynn said. "It sends a strong message."

"Liverpool in a couple of days."

"Yes, then Oxford, Newcastle, and Edinburgh. Back to London in time for Christmas."

"Mid-December, if I remember the schedule right," Alfred said, as the bellboy led them into their suite and handed off the key. Alfred pressed a tip into the boy's hand.

Lynn smiled. Alfred was known to be frugal, sometimes to the point of tightwad. But he never shirked when it came to rewarding those providing service. Lynn thought he did it just as much for the shocked look it produced as anything else.

The bellboy slipped out of the door and closed it behind him.

"Just so. Back for the holidays." Lynn knew Alfred had their stops precisely lined up in his head. He rarely forgot anything, especially when it related to the theater. "I wonder when Hamilton will be contacting us again? Before we leave for Liverpool?"

"I have a feeling he's very busy at the moment," Alfred said. "My bet is he'll wait until we're back in London, as he told us. We're here at the Savoy, and that's the most important thing. We have a place to plant ourselves. He's probably contending with housing and food for the locals. According to everything I've heard, the bombings are continuing."

"I know. I see they posted the instructions about seeking shelter, here on the back of the door, if it comes to that."

"And it will come to that, you can be assured."

Lynn hugged herself and shivered. "Horrible to live under such circumstances."

Just then, Hitler reminded them there was a war on.

Lynn didn't recognize the sounds and screeches of German fighters and falling bombs. But she did recognize the wail of sirens, air raid sirens, she was sure. With haste, they checked the paper posted on the back of the door, both of them scanning with more speed than they would read a pitch for an undesirable script. But by the time they reached the point of "Move quickly to the basement, taking only necessities with you," the raid was over, the sirens' sound descending into mere whines as the All Clear whistle sounded. A false alarm? More like a dress rehearsal. Lynn was sure there would be more, and the real thing too.

Lynn dropped onto the divan and put her hands over her face. She drew them down, then clasped her hands in her lap, the fingers so tight, her nails were white. "How do they do it?"

Alfred wrapped his arms around her. "The same as we will. We'll get used to it, Lynnie. I know we will."

She rested her cheek on his chest, her arms tucked tightly between them. "We must, surely." She brightened a bit. "At least we've now read the procedures for air raids. Those directions are seared into my brain."

Alfred chuckled. "You know, once we're back in London after our first tour, we should see where we can help. There must be places to volunteer our services, like we did at the Stage Door Canteen in New York."

"What a great idea, darling!" Lynn regained her composure. "Anything we can do to help relieve the tension of these bombing raids. Even on tour, we can see what others are doing, so we have an idea of what to explore in London."

"I'm sure we'll have no trouble," Alfred said, releasing her and heading for the bathroom. "I, for one, am going to bed."

"The best idea yet, Alfred," Lynn concurred. "We can start fresh in the morning."

~9~

Within a week, all arrangements for touring were set, and the Lunts hit the road. With the blessing and guidance of the British military authorities, and under the authority of the USO Camp Show, they set off a country-wide tour of military installations and civilian theaters, meeting and entertaining as they polished the play before opening in London. From Bournemouth to Aberdeen, from Bristol to Newcastle, as Alfred crowed, troops training for the invasion of Europe and those back from the front, as well as the local population, were glad for the offerings of the Lunts.

They were both elated at audience responses and convinced that their message of hope in the face of evil was the right thing to mount. The Brits embraced the chance to let down their hair and weep. Sometimes, the sniffing and snuffling from the audience was audible on stage. It was a catharsis for audiences throughout the land. The message of "We know what you are going through, and you can endure," buoyed the Lunts, as well as their audiences, night after night.

After all the admirers that crowded their dressing room after performances finally disappeared, they took time to decompress.

"It happened again, Alfred," Lynn said, "the audience was drenched, everyone was weeping so much. As often as it happens, I am always amazed and humbled."

"We thought the Americans cried a lot at the plight of that family. But I think the Brits have exceeded that," Alfred said. "I don't think they can let down their defenses even at home, much less in public. But in the theater in the dark, they can let go of that stiff upper lip and let the tears flow."

Lynn leaned in toward the dressing table mirror. She swiped the stage makeup off her cheeks and began attending to her eyes, first gently pulling off the false eyelashes. "We too are adjusting to keeping the despair at bay, just as they already have. They lived through that horrible Blitz in 1940." She shook her head and sighed. "I honestly don't know how they've held on so long. The stress is worse than opening night nerves."

Alfred nodded. He took off his dressing gown, exchanging it for a shirt waiting for him on a wall hook.

Lynn closed her eyes and stretched. She ran a hand up her neck, tilting her chin. "Ah!" The tension born of the intense stage performance released. "You were magnificent tonight, Alfred."

"Was I?" He shook his head and bent to finish buttoning his shirt. He tucked it into his pants, pulled up his suspenders, and blew out a breath of exasperation.

Lynn recognized the sign and jumped into the gap. "No, Alfred, you were right on the mark."

"I don't think so. I could breathe more into that role. I just–"

"My darling, you are always far too harsh on yourself. Look at the raves from our guests that came backstage. Stunning, that's what you were," Lynn said. *That's what you always are. Always.* But that remained unspoken. This was one of those post-performance rituals, reassuring him that he really was magnificent. He put his whole heart and soul into a role, and still felt he came up short. It was a good thing she was around to bolster his flagging ego.

Years before, they demanded that they work only together, never in separate plays. It was written into all of their contracts. Lynn was convinced she was the only thing standing between Alfred and either an ulcer or a heart attack. In turn, he doted on her, telling everyone who asked, and often those who didn't, that she was the most fascinating woman he ever met. Like a beautiful pair of carriage horses, they might be different breeds, colors, or temperaments, yet when in harness together–which for them was always–they presented a tandem picture of perfection.

The weeks wore on. Oxford, Newcastle, Edinburgh. More audiences sniffling and weeping. More positive responses to the stage family moving from passive observation of invasion of their country, to stalwart support of the war effort through the son's enlistment and the father's medical skills. Overall, rave reviews spread like wildfire and drew in audiences. Many shows were booked for military personnel, but civilians found their way in also.

Finally, the Lunts arrived back in London shortly before Christmas. Back to the Savoy Hotel, where Alfred could cook many of their meals after prowling markets, careful to use ration cards wisely.

After the play's triumphs they experienced on tour, they were anxious to mount *There Shall Be No Night* in London. They took up theatrical residence in the Aldwych, grateful to be planted in one spot, one theater, for the duration. There would be no escape to America if things got tough. They were in England for as long as it took. They would stay until the war was over.

A few days after their return, they had the chance to experience the joys of the Savoy's air raid shelter in the basement. By this time, they knew the routine, having encountered similar situations on the road.

When the sirens began, Lynn popped up from the desk where she was composing letters to the folks back home. She dropped her pen and headed for the bathroom.

"Lynnie! Come on!" Alfred hollered, sliding on his shoes. "There's no time for makeup now!"

"I'll be right there," she called. "The public deserves my very best, and that's what they're going to get." She attached false eyelashes in a flash, and swiped on lipstick. A bit of rouge and one last sweep of a brush to tame errant strands of hair and she was ready to meet her fans.

She dashed out of the bathroom, slid her feet into shoes, and grabbed her purse.

Alfred was struggling into his coat. "You're supposed to leave everything!" she called. She recognized the irony, considering she took time for makeup and still managed to snatch her purse. She headed for the door without slowing a step.

Stepping out into the corridor was like joining a school of salmon desperate to get upstream. Luckily, everyone was going the same direction. The elevators were far too small, and couldn't be used during air raids anyway, so the Lunts remained part of the mob making its way downstairs in the conventional manner, albeit at a more frantic pace, even though the stairways were clogged with guests.

The clattering stopped as they all funneled into the Savoy's air raid shelter. The doors closed and they were all transported into the refined caring world of a first-class hotel. Along one wall stretched a line of cubicles. From what they could see, each contained a bed and an armchair. Waiters and even nurses made their way among the guests, making sure everyone would have a place to sleep. Even mattresses on the floor farther down the shelter were fitted with sheets and blankets. Beyond that were enclosed toilets for Gents and Ladies, though they remained without the customary staff on hand. At least they were private.

Opposite the cubicles, the wall boasted a bar, stocked with basic liquors, though with not quite the selection of the upstairs bar. Beyond the bar, chefs and busboys were setting up a buffet of foods and non-alcoholic drinks. A coffee urn, several actually, awaited those who needed a boost. But most guests made for the tea station. The choice of teas was limited, but certainly sufficed to bolster spirits. Hotel personnel offered food and drink, as well as calmed guests who were agitated, and reassured those who needed it.

Time stretched out and people settled into a routine. Since there was a gramophone, a number of couples danced. Those interested in news above ground clustered around a radio, set up far enough away from the music so they could hear without disturbance. One woman pulled out a knitting project from a large bag. "For the new grandchild," she announced to anyone who asked.

Several groups broke off and began parlor games. The staff also distributed board games for anyone wishing that diversion. Of course, there were also knots of drinkers, those Brits who got over the shock of drinking somewhere other than home or in an established pub.

Lynn and Alfred experienced raids as they toured, so Lynn had no problem imagining the night deepening above them here in the city, the sky exploding into bursts of light from bombs. Searchlights would stab the air in their search for German fighters and bombers. Lynn could even hear the muffled rat-a-tat of the ack-ack guns as they fired into the sky. This was worse than in the outlying towns. London was heavily targeted. War was on them, full force.

Yet, life went on in the shelter.

Lynn whispered to Alfred, "It's as if all is well. It appears that some see this as an adventure, not even an inconvenience." She cuddled closer to Alfred. "Will we get this blasé, I wonder?"

-10-

They did become blasé. A bit.

Lynn acclimated to the sounds and vibrations of bombs. Sitting at the desk in their hotel suite, she could almost ignore the sounds and sirens enough to compose a reasonably calm letter to Hattie. Almost. But after another night spent in the Savoy's air raid shelter in the basement, cramped and cold in spite of the amenities offered by the hotel, she rebelled.

Once back in their suite, she turned to Alfred. "It's just breaking dawn, and I haven't slept all night. It's difficult enough in normal times to get enough rest to really give our play my all. This is almost impossible." She smoothed her hands across her rumpled hair.

"I know, Lynnie. I can't sleep either with all that snoring sounding like an incoming train." Alfred came out of the bathroom and handed her a plate of coddled eggs with a side of bacon.

Lynn grinned. "I'm glad you're getting some use out of that hot plate, Alfred. This is certainly less harried than the air raid shelter. I think my blood pressure is finally dropping to normal."

"We must speak to the manager," Alfred said. "Maybe we can stay up here when the sirens go off."

Lynn sighed and rolled her eyes. "From your lips to his ears." She tucked into her eggs.

After breakfast, they sought out Hugh Wontner, the Savoy's General Manager.

He led Lynn and Alfred to his private office. "Mr. Lunt. Miss Fontanne. Please forgive my effrontery, but you two are precious to Londoners. I myself want to protect you as much as possible. It would be best if you went down into our well-equipped air raid shelter. We made over the Abraham Lincoln banqueting hall for just that purpose. The shelter can hold several hundred guests, if necessary." He was clearly trying to dissuade them from staying in their suite during air raids.

Alfred held up a hand. "We appreciate all that the Savoy does for us, but we feel that we must follow the government's advice on the posters we see. 'Keep Calm and Carry On.' A good piece of advice, don't you think?"

Wontner tightened his lips a bit, but Lynn could see that he was too much of a gentleman to actually frown. "If you were here during the Blitz in 1940, you would see many people that didn't believe the city would ever be bombed. At first, the Luftwaffe struck airfields and industry on the periphery, not central London itself, and not civilians, certainly. So, the end of August seemed to prove the nay-sayers' complacency. However, by mid-September, Hitler gave orders to bomb the East End, and then to move into central London itself, bombing willy-nilly, it seemed, without regard to what lay below. The Savoy's roof was hit that November. Why, even Buckingham Palace was hit twice. That destruction won over many of the cynics. But human as we are..." Wontner held out his hands, palms up, and tilted his head. "...hoping against all odds, many felt that bombs would surely not touch them. They were wrong."

Lynn recognized the truth of what he said. London remained a shambles from the Blitz three years before. "We understand, believe me, we do. It could be dangerous to ignore the sirens. But part of our mission here is to show that we do not fear Hitler."

Wontner harumphed, though it rumbled into a discreet cough.

"You are right," Alfred said. "The bombings are terrifying, especially when the explosions hit close. But we must carry on as normally as we can. We provide a refuge from the storm, you see."

Lynn added, "Your citizens have cleared areas of rubble, and attend church where the towers have been destroyed, and congregate in the pubs still standing. Those too are places of refuge. The stamina and courage of Londoners during this time is most heartening." She leaned in and set a hand on Wontner's arm. We feel obliged, and privileged too, to match their fortitude. We are honored to do so."

"The proverbial British stiff upper lip," Alfred said. "Please do not deny us the ability to serve as models for those who look up to us for strength. Strength comes from what we do on stage, but strength from our actions off the stage as well."

Wontner nodded, a mere tip of the chin, but it was enough for Lynn to see surrender. "Of course, the decision remains with you. But the hotel and I have an obligation to warn all our patrons. We relinquish all responsibility if you decide to stay upstairs. But I see, you must do what will serve you best. We will, of course, accept whatever you decide to do." He folded his hands in front of him.

"Your concern is very much appreciated," Lynn said.

"Consider your duties fulfilled," Alfred said. "If there are times we feel unsafe in our suite, we will gratefully join you in the Savoy's shelter."

"You are entirely welcome," Wontner said. "With that, I fear I must return to my other duties. In these trying times, we must carry on."

"And you do it in fine fashion," Lynn said, turning to leave the office.

After wending their way through the crowds in the lobby, military and otherwise, they slipped into the elevator and headed back to their rooms.

Alfred closed the door behind them and said, "Of course, the man doesn't recommend us staying in our suite. I know he foregoes all responsibilities if we decide to stay upstairs, but he does seem to understand what a toll the bombing is taking on people's personal and professional lives, ours included." Alfred raised his eyebrows at her. "What do you think?"

"I don't think, I know." Lynn released her chignon from its hairpins and shook her hair loose. "I don't want to spend another night down there, if I can help it. If, during an air raid, Lady Oxford can sit in the Thames Foyer in a long white evening gown with a train, and wearing leather boots, playing bridge and chatting with any and all, then so can I." She chuckled, then turned serious and took Alfred's hands. "What do *you* think?"

"I'm with you, darling." He pulled her into his arms. "We'll be fine."

She chose not to check the expression on his face. Better to stick to her guns. A rather unfortunate phrase to pop into her mind, she thought.

They decided not to allow the air raid sirens to govern every aspect of their lives, and opted to stay in their suite.

But when they were at the theater, the Aldwych insisted that they go to the nearest shelter when the bombings came too close. For weeks, that was the decision of the theater management, not the Lunts, who chafed under the order to evacuate.

One morning, a knock on the door startled them. "Are we expecting anyone?" Alfred headed for the door.

Lynn shook her head. "No, but I wish that man Hamilton would show up. The State Department back in New York seemed adamant that we meet him and work with him somehow."

Her wish appeared to be a command, as Alfred opened the door to reveal, who else but James Hamilton. "Ah! At last we meet the elusive man again."

"Come in, come in!" Alfred swept his arm out in a gesture of welcome. "We wondered when you would reappear."

"I've been consumed with work," James said. "Too much to do and not enough hands to do it."

"The perfect segue," Alfred said. "Lynn and I were talking not long ago about what we could do to help." He led James deeper into the sitting room to meet with Lynn.

"Do sit down," Lynn said, patting the couch next to her.

Alfred took a chair across from them and leaned forward, resting his arms on his thighs and clasping his hands. "Tell us how we can help."

James put his briefcase on the floor and joined Lynn. He set his hands on his lap and took a deep breath. "I'm glad you asked. We can use air raid wardens, for one.'

"What does that entail?" Alfred asked.

"Well, you get to wear a helmet with a big W on the front." Laugh lines appeared around his eyes. "One of the fashion statements of the war."

"I've seen the wardens at work," Lynn said. "That would mean we would hand out gas masks and guide people to shelters. Are you a warden yourself?"

"No, I'm a fire marshal, which has more responsibility, but it allows me to get all over the city. My wife is at the British Library, but she's also a spotter, so she's out some nights helping work the spotlights so the men firing the ack-ack guns can bring down the German planes.

"But a warden is different," James went on. "It's more than just handing out gas masks. They are assigned one of any number of tasks. They are responsible for passing on any information about bomb damage as well as investigating any reports of unexploded bombs." At Lynn's expression of horror, he reassured, "Oh, they don't do anything with unexploded ordnance, but they do report it to the authorities so they can defuse whatever was discovered. Besides that, many carry a pike to probe any debris for possible survivors."

"And if they find any?" Alfred asked.

"Wardens have first aid kits, certainly, and can administer help where they can. Of course, they are the front line of a network of people looking out for our citizens," James said. "We'd find you a good fit as a warden, and assign you to that. Plenty of ways to help. But there are other opportunities as well, if you feel your availability is too limited." He sat back. "For example, the hospitals are really desperate for help too."

Lynn lifted her shoulders. "I don't think I'm cut out for that kind of work. I'm...well, I'm not very good around blood and such."

"That's fine," James said. "We can use you both as wardens." He turned to Alfred and raised his eyebrows.

"Perfect," Alfred said. "Sign us up. We can become wardens. Can you make the arrangements for us, please?"

"Of course. I'd be delighted." James leaned over and picked up his briefcase. He hugged it to himself and cleared his throat. "There is something else."

I knew it, Lynn thought. *Our State Department man's mannerisms just reeked of an underlying motive for meeting Mr. Hamilton over here.* "Mmm? What else concerns you, James?"

James twisted in his seat a bit. "Well, no maids cleaning your suite today, I see." He brought his glance back to the Lunts, and lay an index finder along his cheek. He appeared to be pointing to his ear.

Ah, Lynn thought, *no ears to hear what we say. But pay attention and watch. He clearly has something to impart that he doesn't want anyone else to hear. Whatever it is will probably be tucked into ordinary conversation. This ought to be interesting.*

Alfred sat back in his chair and set his arms on the rests, his eyes firmly fixed on James.

Lynn recognized the signs. Alfred was totally engaged and focused on the man sitting across from him. The whole atmosphere felt charged.

Though both of the Lunts memorized words in a script, they were even more attuned to the spaces between the words and the lines. Nuances that couldn't be put down on paper, couldn't even necessarily be directed. Nuances that had to be felt, intuited, drawn out from what wasn't said, as much as from what was written on the page. Or said, in this case. She sat up straight.

"We need your help," James said. He stopped, set his briefcase flat on his lap, and fixed his gaze on Alfred

"Yes?" Alfred waited.

Lynn knew it was her turn to prime the pump. "Tell us how we can help." She deliberately didn't add "you" or anything else that would impinge on his answer. She sent James one of her best smiles, the one that also didn't break eye contact.

"I really hate to impose, Miss Fontanne," James said, his brow creasing into worry lines.

Lynn noted the "Miss Fontanne." Hamilton's laugh lines around his eyes were gone, his mouth pulled tighter than it was a moment ago when discussing air raid wardens. Such formality with her name surely indicated that he probably needed something to do with the war effort. Something clandestine, perhaps. From her keen observation of people wherever she went, Lynn knew this was more than a shot in the dark.

Hamilton filled his cheeks and pushed out a breath. "You could do us a great favor. I know you've been looking for another stagehand..."

We've been doing nothing of the sort, Lynn thought. Her attention sharpened.

"Yes, indeed," Alfred said, clinching Lynn's conviction that Alfred too realized the import of this conversation. "Have you someone in mind?"

"A young friend of a friend, who isn't medically able to join up, needs something to keep him occupied, keep him from doing something other than taking care of his Bulldog." A very light emphasis on that last word.

Sanctioned by Churchill himself, Lynn concluded. "Of course we can take him on. What's his name?" She assumed James would create a false name.

"Philip Arbuthnot, but everyone calls him Pip. Don't worry, he's a quick study."

"We will treat him as–"Alfred said.

"–one of our theater family," Lynn finished.

"Do you know him well, by the way?" Alfred asked. "I only ask, because if you don't have time to tell us our volunteer jobs, you can send it with him."

"Yes," Lynn said. "We know how busy you are. So, if you do see him now and again, and need to give us more direction about our volunteer efforts, you could get all that information to us very easily, and save yourself a trip all the way over here." From where, she had no clear idea, but that wasn't the thrust here anyway.

James nodded. "A capital idea, Miss Fontanne."

Alfred chimed in. "And if we are stuck with where we're supposed to be or what else we should be doing, we can ask Pip. No reason to barge on into your full-up calendar. Makes both our lives easy. To say nothing of his welcome work as our new stagehand. That'll take some pressure off our overworked crew."

Running off at the mouth, again, Alfred, Lynn thought. *A good diversion.*

"We do cross paths occasionally," Hamilton said, his voice noncommittal. He turned in his seat to face Lynn. "But say–"

Lynn recognized a change of tack. She stretched out her legs and crossed her ankles, the perfect picture of a relaxed listener. She was far from that.

"So, Miss Fontanne, how are the audiences at your performances?" James said. "I'll bet you have lots of returnees, people that come back again and again, just because they love your theater work so much."

"Oh, I suspect there are. I try to keep a sharp eye out for anyone who loves us enough to come back to the same play more than once."

"More than a few times, I'll bet, you two are that good."

Alfred chuckled. "They come to see Lynnie more than to see me, I'm afraid. I'm just the bombastic ol' actor who gets to hug the beautiful leading lady."

Leading astray, as usual, Lynn thought. *What a darling husband I have! And what a team we make.*

Alfred sent her a smile that said they would fill in the blanks later. She dazzled him with the same response.

"My friends have seen your play," James said, "and they rhapsodized over both of you. There seems to be one or another attending every performance. They especially like the scene with the two of you discussing your son. It's strange to see you, Miss Fontanne, in a housedress and that red apron."

Lynn's ears perked up like a hunting dog on point. Housedress and red apron? What's the message he's sending? Or asking? She looked to Alfred, but he raised eyebrows that said, "I'm not sure." She tilted her head and cleared her throat. "Well, you know, a blue apron would never do. A blue apron would send the wrong message. It's a cold color." Now, if that didn't pique his interest, nothing would. This, perhaps, could be another vehicle to put out a signal that they found, or heard...something, and needed Hamilton to come. Would he catch it?

James was staring at her. But then he laughed, a long and deep laugh. But his eyes never closed. Lynn recognized the implication. Yes, it was clear. If they needed him, she was to wear the blue apron, not the red.

"I do believe you are the most delightful woman," James said. "I love your wit."

"I tell everyone she is the most fascinating woman I've ever met," Alfred said, sealing the deal.

"Well, I must be going. Lots to do," James said. "Keep your audiences riveted, as you always do. I know you can reach the boxes in the theater. I admire that. I wish I could project myself that far. Plenty of times to use that in what I do out there on the streets." He winked so quickly, Lynn almost missed it. "My wife and I hope to take in one of your performances, a matinee or early evening performance, perhaps. But for now, must run."

James stretched out his hand to shake Alfred's. Lynn did the same. "I'll be in touch about your volunteer choices."

"Perfect," Alfred said.

"Done and done," Lynn added.

James grasped his briefcase and stood up. He leaned in and pulled the two of them close to whisper, "Watch what you say. Don't discuss this out loud. Walls still have ears." He stepped back and started for the door, followed by Lynn and Alfred. His voice went up to its normal volume. "I know how you two can get while rehearsing. And don't make too much noise doing...other things."

Alfred laughed and opened the door to shepherd him out. He closed the door and leaned back against it. He raised his eyebrows. Leading Lynn back into the middle of the sitting room, Alfred's voice dropped to a whisper. "He's obviously looking for a member of the Fifth Column, those Nazi sympathizers, who would do anything to see England overrun."

"Clearly," Lynn said, matching his tone. "That man–assuming it is a man–apparently loves theater. Not only that, but has been to see us multiple times. We must sharpen our eyes, Alfred."

"He must sit in one of the boxes, the way James was talking."

"Yes. When we do curtain calls, that's where we must look. Perhaps someone who gives us a standing ovation from his box."

"Easy enough, considering sometimes we have a dozen calls. That should give us ample time to ferret out a familiar face."

Lynn said, "James said there's always a 'friend' in attendance. That means someone is always watching us, and can get a message of the blue apron to him, without exposing us."

"What that really means, is that there will be a member of the SOE in every audience." At Lynn's questioning look, he added, "Special Operations Executive, the British intelligence service."

Lynn shook her head. "Where do you pick up all these details, Alfred? You are a veritable encyclopedia."

"I listen at keyholes, Lynnie."

She laughed, knowing he was joking. But he had the most uncanny ability of drawing people out in a conversation. Of course, so did she, thanks to theater training. Listen and watch, because you never knew when something could be used on stage.

Lynn set one hand on Alfred's chest, "So, we're spies now. How very interesting."

~11~

Christmas was rather uneventful. Antoinette, on leave from the Land Girls for the holiday, managed to squeeze some champagne out of someone, she wouldn't say who. Alfred, always enterprising, haunted the markets and stored away a motley selection of canned goods. He finished up the month's ration book for sugar and flour. He humbled himself to beg the hotel kitchen for eggs, raised in the hotel's very own chicken coop on the outskirts of the city. A fine, although small, cake emerged as a result. He created magic with canned meat, while their friends promised to share rations.

At the last moment, just a day before Christmas, a package arrived from Alfred's mother, Hattie, back at their estate in Wisconsin.

"Chocolate! Alfred, look, chocolate! Wherever did Hat manage to find such a trove?" Lynn was ecstatic.

Alfred pulled a small bag out of the box and held it up to his nose. "Coffee! The real stuff." He set it aside and dug back into the box. "Look, Lynnie, she didn't forget you. A nice packet of Earl Grey tea."

Lynn sighed and accepted the tea, pressing it to her lips and closing her eyes.

Alfred peered into the box once more. He laughed long and hard. "I don't know where she thinks we are, but look, she stuck wool socks down in the bottom."

"I don't know about you, Alfred, but I am grateful beyond measure. Finally, my feet will be warm. I'm taking a pair to my dressing room. They don't turn the heat on in the theater."

"Once everyone gets in, the place heats up nicely," Alfred said.

"Yes, for the audience," Lynn said, pulling a long face. "But my arms are blue by the time I get offstage. At least now I'll be able to make a mad dash for those wool socks and bring my feet back to life."

"Thank Hattie for small favors," Alfred said, pulling out multiple pairs of socks.

"Big favors, don't you mean?" Lynn's comment ended the conversation, as a knock on their door indicated their guests' arrival.

So, Christmas, though sparse and rather quiet, passed, and New Year's Eve handed them off into 1944. Fireworks were limited to explosions and fires from the German bombs. Thank you, Hitler.

* * *

January slipped into February, and on into March, and the blue apron sat at the back of the prop table, waiting.

Early in the war, and during the 1940-41 Blitz, the sound of German Luftwaffe fighters and the whistles of the falling bombs sent people into a panic. But after that horror, because of the successes of the Royal Air Force, there was a lull.

Until shortly after the Lunts arrived.

The Baby Blitz began in earnest right after Lynn and Alfred's Christmas celebration. Once again, the Germans appeared in force in the London skies. Fighter planes screamed, bombs let out with satanic whistles, ack-ack guns returned fire from emplacements around London. The city was on fire from incendiary bombs. Bodies were buried as buildings collapsed. A man could take his dog for a walk and come home to find his home demolished, and his wife, whom he'd left cleaning up the kitchen after dinner, crushed under the rubble.

Most nights, blackout was imposed early, six or seven in the evening. Performances of *There Shall Be No Night* were forced to begin earlier as well. Matinees begun at three were over a mere half-hour before the evening performance began at six. Lynn and Alfred never ate between performances anyway, preferring to dine after the last curtain, so the schedule change didn't alter their habits.

What was frustrating was the mandatory evacuation when the sound and fury got close enough for the air raid sirens to howl. That wail came one evening, right in the middle of the second act. The stage manager rushed onstage and interrupted the scene. He directed everyone out of the building and across the street, down into the Aldwych Tube Station, a massive location remade at night into an air raid shelter that could hold well over a thousand people.

Alfred gripped Lynn's arm as they hustled across the street. "Stay close, Lynnie!" he hollered over the sounds of war and the cries of terrified civilians. "I don't want to lose you!"

They were swept along, like horses in a stampede, barely able to change direction or keep their footing. At the top of the steps to the Tube entrance, Lynn stumbled, twisting in a grotesque dance in an attempt to regain her balance in the midst of a sea of panicked people. "Alfred! Alfred!" It was all she could get out. Her breath was ragged and swiftly turning to desperate gasps. With barely a moment to go before she would plunge down the steps and into the crowd, surely to be lost to any chance of emerging whole, she felt Alfred grab the back of her dress. He hauled her upright and pressed her between himself and the stairwell's tiled wall.

The crowd flowed past them. Or, to be more accurate, she thought in an odd moment of clarity, through them. She was buffeted and scraped, in spite of Alfred's body protecting her. Together, they worked their way down the stairs, gradually picking up speed to match the rest of the mob so as not to be pushed down and left behind in a bloody heap.

By the time they were able to swing around the corner at the bottom of the stairway, moving out of the mainstream of people, the pulse of the crowd was slowing. Everyone that could get down, was down.

Lynn leaned into Alfred. She tried to hold back her tears, but they leaked out unbidden. "I can't do this, Alfred." She crept back around the corner and collapsed on the bottom step, now blessedly empty of anyone. "I really can't. Imagine if we were separated. I would've been crushed. I was so afraid I wasn't going to make it out alive. If you hadn't been there–"

Alfred dropped down beside her and gathered her in his arms. "I was there, Lynnie. I wasn't about to let go."

"I know, darling, I know. But can you imagine? Over a thousand people crowding down one stairway? One of these times, there will be the devil to pay."

Alfred nodded and kissed the top of her head. "I think we should do the same thing we do at the Savoy."

"Emulate Lady Oxford." That brought a bit of a smile to Lynn's face. "Simply carry on."

"Simply carry on," Alfred agreed. "We'll make it clear to the theater that we must, for everyone's sake, just keep the play going. The play's setting *is* in the middle of a war, after all."

"Oh, the irony," Lynn said, lifting her head from Alfred's embrace. "I'll leave it up to you. I know how persuasive you can be, darling."

Keeping one arm around her shoulders, Alfred settled more firmly on the step. "You're the power behind my words, you know. We'll go in together." He arranged her sweater closer around her shoulders. "As for now–"

"As for now, I'm going nowhere." Lynn freed one hand enough to wave it along the Tube's platform. "Look at them all. There's not one inch of space anywhere. How can anyone sleep, packed in so like sardines in a can? They're even sleeping on the tracks."

"I'd prefer one of those hammocks slung across the tracks, myself," Alfred said, "though it looks like those are set up for the children."

"Not exactly the Savoy shelter, is it?"

"At least, there's a first aid station down here. And I heard they have games stashed somewhere for the children."

"All well and good, but I prefer to stay above ground." Lynn leaned against Alfred. "I'm spending the night right here, next to you. I hope you don't plan on trying out one of those hammocks." A small attempt at humor to show him she was back to normal.

"I'm six-foot two, Lynnie. I'd be hanging over the edges." They both chuckled at the absurd image. "It looks like everyone is bedded down. It's getting pretty quiet."

Lynn could still hear the bombs falling above them, and feel the rumbles of the earth, not from the trains, but from the seismic quakes caused by nearby hits. "It's all right, Alfred. We'll be all right." She closed her eyes and sensed a small frisson of surprise as she felt her body insist on slipping toward sleep, in spite of the hell going on up in the streets.

The very next evening, the Luftwaffe struck again. This time, the audience was primed before the curtain went up. "No need to evacuate," the stage manager came out to explain. "The Lunts insist that the show must go on. If the sirens go off, we will persevere." He might have said more, but the roars of approbation and the applause drowned out anything further.

From then on, for better or worse, the play went forward, with Lynn and Alfred seemingly oblivious to the sounds of planes and anti-aircraft fire, until it seemed that the bombings were meant just for them. Often, when they came out for curtain calls, Alfred would hold up his hands for quiet, and announce, "We'd like to thank Herr Hitler for providing the sound effects tonight." Wry laughter always rang out amid the tragedy of the streets.

One night, an especially loud exchange between air and ground forces had Alfred looking to the sky. He turned to the characters onstage. "The enemy is not very far away." He delivered his line, right on cue. The audience erupted in cheers. It was a moment of catharsis.

~12~

Alfred was restless. Though he was a warden, along with Lynn, it was a position requiring him to do little. In fact, the leaders wouldn't let him do anything dangerous, protecting him. He found a solution rather quickly, however.

"I volunteered at the hospital nearby as an orderly," he told Lynn one morning after disappearing for a walk.

"But everybody knows you, Alfred," she said. "They'll relegate you to the background again. They seem to think we need to be treated like porcelain dolls."

Alfred winked. "I solved that problem. I'm in disguise."

"Oh, come now, Alfred." She scoffed. "You can't go about in makeup."

"No, no, Lynnie," Alfred said. "You know I can become someone else pretty easily. And it doesn't always take makeup either."

Lynn set her hands on her hips. "All right, smarty. What did you come up with this time? The most striking time you did this, you 'became' a Russian count, with a false beard, imperious voice, and one of those big fur hats. Quite impressive, I must admit. You fooled our lifelong grocer."

"Well, yes. Thank you for that fine compliment." Alfred beamed at her. "But this time, I merely changed my name."

"You don't think they'll recognize you anyway at that hospital?" Her tone oozed skepticism.

"They are far too busy to know who we are," Alfred said. "Or to care, at this point. Oh, Lynnie, they really need me. So many casualties. Some from the bombings here, of course, but also some of their patients are men sent back from the front." He shook his head and pressed his lips together.

"I know you can help, Alfred. When you step in, you always make a difference. You're certainly not afraid of hard work either." She reached up and gave him a pat on the cheek. "You said you changed your name. So, who are you now?"

He grinned, leaned over and whispered in her ear.

She burst into a peal of laughter. "Karolos? You gave them the name of your character from our play?" She pressed her hands to her lips to control the giggles. "That is hilarious." She tsk-tsked. "Well, that should take care of anyone bothering you for an autograph. You are assuming, of course, that nobody has time to go to the theater."

"They are up to their ears in work, Lynnie." Alfred's voice was serious. "If they have seen the play, then the joke will be on me."

That very night, they had a visitor backstage after the performance. That was nothing new. People flocked to them, offering thanks for the message of hope, for choosing to fight when all seemed hopeless, for triumph in the face of evil. Even though rationing was tightly regulated, sometimes a small gift of chocolate or tea, or even sugar would be handed to them. But this visitor came to offer apologies.

The Lunts welcomed the man into their dressing room. "Oh, no, it's never too late to meet with our fans," Lynn said, gesturing him in. "Don't apologize. Come in for a moment, at least. Alfred will be right back. He just went to get out of his costume."

At that moment, Alfred swept in, tying the belt on his dressing gown. He was busy with the knot and not paying attention to their guest.

"Oh, Mr. Lunt!" the man gushed. "I am so very sorry–"

Alfred looked up. "Good heavens, it's Dr. Martin! Lynnie, this is the man I work for on the mornings I'm at the hospital." He reached out and shook the doctor's hand.

Dr. Martin appeared to have been struck dumb for a moment. Finally, he blurted, "Why didn't you tell me you were Alfred Lunt?"

Lynn started to laugh. "So, this is the man you've been deceiving, Alfred. How charming!"

"I–I–I saw the name in the playbill, the name you're using at the hospital. Then you came on stage, and I thought, *This* is the man I set to emptying bedpans? I simply couldn't believe it!"

Alfred waved his hand in a dismissive gesture. "Nothing to worry about, nothing at all. But say, how did you like the play? I think I should have done that last scene a little more–"

"Just ignore him, doctor," Lynn interrupted. "He's always looking for ways to make it better. Always self-critical. But he was wonderful, don't you think?"

"Marvelous, just marvelous," Dr. Martin said. "I loved the line, something about throwing books."

Alfred took on the character of the intellectual doctor he played. "'When the enemies use force, you can't throw books at them.'"

"So apropos, don't you think?" Dr. Martin said. He and Alfred sailed off on a discussion of the necessity at times of going to war.

Lynn stepped in as she saw Alfred's shoulders droop just a bit. "Gentlemen, I think it's time to call it a night. We are all weary. You, especially, Dr. Martin. You carry a heavy load."

"I do what I can, Miss Fontanne. You're right, of course. I didn't mean to keep you this long."

With thanks all around, they topped off the evening. With Dr. Martin's exit, Lynn and Alfred closed up shop and called a good night to the stage manager who was waiting to lock up behind them. Alfred offered Lynn his arm, and they set off for the short walk to the Savoy.

"The skies are quiet tonight, for once," Lynn said.

"Yes, but Hitler seems to be stepping up the attacks," Alfred said. "I just have a feeling we're going to be seeing James Hamilton again soon. Something is in the air, and it isn't just the Germans."

Lynn squeezed his arm. "You and your wit, Alfred. Sometimes I wonder..." But she didn't wonder about this premonition. She felt the same. The tension was palpable. What next?

-13-

As March advanced, the bombings became more intense, and seemed to be more directed as well. Lynn and Alfred stuck to their decision to keep the show running, in spite of the air raid sirens. It gave a deep verisimilitude to the scenes of the play, written about the Nazis invading Greece, coming closer and closer to the family whose husband, an academic convinced that he could find the philosophical "power to conquer bestiality," finally discovered that words weren't enough to conquer evil. Lynn was sure the audience sometimes thought they made up lines as the situation demanded, considering what was going on in real life. But no, they never altered a line. The play spoke to the beleaguered citizens in the seats, showing them the rightness of their own war.

Everybody, including Pip, warned them of the dangers, but Lynn and Alfred both assured everyone that it was imperative to bolster morale where they could, and the theater was their best venue. Eventually, the doomsday sayers simply sighed and backed off.

The truth of the danger came home very abruptly one evening when a buzz bomb hit the theater itself.

The foyer and audience were spared, but the stage was another story. Alfred and Lynn were in the middle of the play when the blast occurred, hurling one actor, who was waiting backstage, right out the stage door. Scenery began falling. Everyone onstage came out of their roles. This was not a time the show could go on.

"Alfred!" Lynn screamed as a section of scenery detached itself and began to fall just above him.

He looked up just in time to lift his arms and catch the flat. Others rushed to his aid. The scenery was hoisted back into place, and secured enough to be safe.

Lynn whirled to Alfred. She could feel the blood draining from her face. What she saw caught her up short. There stood Alfred, a determined look on his face. She could read his thoughts as clear as if he said them aloud. They must go on with the play. Get back into the role. Remember your lines. Restore normality. She settled immediately, and silently sent back the same message, knowing he would understand. She stood up straight, clasped her hands in front of her mouth, and took a single step toward him. Rehearsed over and over, it all dropped into place.

Alfred, back in character as well, moved to her and grasped her hands. He delivered the well-rehearsed line. "Are you all right, darling?"

The theater exploded in cheers and whoops, feet stomping, tears and laughter. With a sideways glance, Lynn could see every single person on their feet, clapping and waving. She felt that the audience wasn't sure if that line was part of the play, or if Alfred adlibbed it. Either way, it fit the situation perfectly. A pause just long enough for her to nod at Alfred, then a bit longer for the hubbub to subside. The action resumed.

That night, no one left the theater until after the last curtain call. Lynn counted thirteen before they could escape backstage for good.

Until others assured them of the massive damage all over the city, they were leaning into paranoia. Were they themselves being targeted?

They questioned Pip, being unable to reach Hamilton directly, and had no clear answers. "Send Hamilton," they told Pip, who assured them the message would be delivered the following morning, if not possible that night. It would have to do.

When the Lunts returned to the Savoy, they discovered almost every window in the hotel shattered. Hitler's Luftwaffe hit not only their theater, but their hotel.

Lynn fretted. "Where is Hamilton? Something is happening here, and I feel outside the loop."

"I agree," Alfred said. "We need to touch base with him soon."

"Pip has been in and out after performances with flowers from admirers, but he hasn't indicated that he's found any more about the man they're watching."

"We know they have their eye on one box. It's always filled with ministers and their guests, so I think they know who the theater aficionado is." Alfred shook his head. "They don't seem to have any clear subversive activity to hang on...well, I don't know who exactly of that bunch is their target. It could be almost any one of them."

Lynn nodded. "When the house lights go up for our curtain calls, I scan everywhere, and, you're right. That one box has several guests that attend more often than others. It must be one of those men. I just wish we knew who it was for sure. Maybe we could help somehow."

"Once Pip secures a positive name," Alfred said. "What with the increase in attacks, something must be going down. Is our suspect involved in that, or..." He raised his arms and dropped them. A pretty clear sign of defeat. He headed toward the window, but was stopped by the shards of glass on the floor below the sill. The heavy drapes, closed because of the enforced blackout, protected the broken pieces from shooting too far into the room. Most of the window glass was pulled outward from the suction of the bomb's pressure pulse, but the interior damage was still extensive. The hotel already nailed plywood across the opening, which wouldn't keep out the spring winds and cold very well, but it was better than nothing.

"Be careful, Alfred," Lynn said. "Come back here and sit down."

He turned and joined her, dropping into an upholstered chair with its back to the window. "I hope you're ready to cuddle tonight, because my feet are already getting cold."

Lynn chuckled. "I'm so glad you haven't lost your sense of humor."

Alfred sent her a wry smile. "Acting, darling. Pure and simple."

* * *

A cream envelope, embossed with the royal seal, arrived at the Savoy for the Lunts in early April, not long after the theater and hotel scare. An invitation to Windsor for lunch with King George VI and the royal family, and a performance of *There Shall Be No Night*. Or, as was gently suggested, a selection of scenes, should their time be so short as to preclude the entire play.

Lynn was a bundle of nerves as she prepared her wardrobe for their command performance with the king and queen. She almost emptied her armoire, first holding up a garment to herself and turning this way and that in front of the pier mirror in an attempt to determine if this dress, that suit, this ensemble would be fitting to meet the royals. Flinging dresses across the bed, she finally gave up in frustration. "Alfred, I need help!" she called into the bathroom, where Alfred was shaving. "I can't decide!"

"Be right out," Alfred called.

She plopped down on the bed and fingered one piece after another while she waited. When Alfred emerged from the bathroom, her mouth dropped open. "Oh! What? You're wearing your uniform pants! Is that appropriate? Alfred?" She was mystified. "I know, the Camp Shows, in conjunction with the military, issued us military uniforms. I guess it makes sense for their entertainers. We're not sent to the front yet, but many of the others are."

"Our chance could be coming, Lynnie," Alfred said, stretching his suspenders up over his shoulders and reaching into his closet for his tunic. "We've put in to go over."

Lynn pouted. "It feels like they don't think we'd be as much a hit as Hope and Dietrich."

Alfred dismissed that doubt with a wave of his hands. "Don't worry. We have plenty to draw from. And everyone knows us. Give it time."

"Well, in the meantime, I've got to get dressed." She sighed. "I can't really do much to increase the style of these uniforms."

Alfred came over and pulled her to her feet. "Here. Help me with top button. You're so much better than I am." He stood, ready for her attentions.

She obliged. "You always look so dapper, Alfred, no matter what you put on."

He leaned down and planted a kiss on her lips. "As do you. You'd think Schiaparelli designed it when you put it on."

Her laugh sounded like bells. "All right, all right, Mr. Style. I'll match you."

"And raise me, along with you."

"At least, Alfred, the uniform will show our solidarity with the Allies and with the royal family, who has been doing their own part to help, by the way," Lynn said.

A knock on the door had Lynn reaching for her dressing gown and securing the sash as Alfred went to answer the summons.

Lynn expected to see a driver ready to sweep them away. But it was Pip.

Alfred drew the young man into the room. "What brings you here?" A chuckle from Alfred. "Don't you get enough of us in the theater?"

The look on Pip's face worried Lynn and stopped any further comments from Alfred. "What is it, Pip?" Lynn asked. "Come sit down." She swept to the couch, then patted the cushion next to her.

Pip perched on the edge, as Alfred settled into a nearby chair. "I'm sorry to bother you as you're about to head off to Windsor." At Alfred's dismissive wave, he went on. "I couldn't get to you at the theater, so..."

Lynn and Alfred both nodded. Backstage often became crowded, and sometimes the Lunts left with the last of their visitors.

Pip fidgeted, clasping and unclasping his hands, pulling on his fingers, pursing his lips. "The blue apron," he said.

That got Lynn's attention. She noticed Alfred sit upright and lean forward, his hands on his knees, so close, his knees touched Pip's. She drew herself up and nodded at Pip to continue.

"Our friend will be with you the next day." Pip's voice was reassuring. "The man they think is the collaborator's been at the play multiple times."

Lynn set her fingers on her mouth. She did understand that the less they knew, the less they could reveal.

Pip nodded. "Something is on the brink."

"How can we help?" Alfred asked.

"This, to JH," Pip said. He waited a moment, then added, "You're right, the forest is beautiful this time of year."

"Forest." Alfred said. "The one at Windsor?"

Lynn kicked his ankle. "I'm sure it is. Lovely, that is."

"As I told you: the forest is beautiful this time of year." Pip leaned so far forward that Lynn was afraid their foreheads would collide. "Just that way, just those words."

Lynn held up a single finger. "Just so."

Alfred licked his lips and nodded.

"You won't forget?" Pip's voice betrayed a touch of fear and more than a touch of doubt. "You've not done this kind of thing before."

Alfred and Lynn smiled at each other. Lynn said, "We are professionals, Pip." She added in a normal voice. "The forest *is* beautiful this time of year. I can't wait to visit."

Pip looked more relaxed. He stood, strode to the door, turned before either of them had a chance to follow. He saluted, opened the door and was gone.

Lynn looked at Alfred, who closed the door behind Pip and rejoined Lynn. "Well, that was intriguing. It looks like our role now has a life of its own."

Alfred blew out a long stream of air. "A challenging role, the way it's beginning to look."

"I know how you feel," Lynn said. She untied her dressing gown belt and swept the gown off, dropping it on a chair as she passed. "But right now, we need to get ready for Windsor. They stipulated no props, no lights, no stage makeup." She pulled her Camp Shows uniform out of the armoire. She stepped into the skirt and buttoned and zipped. The military cut of the jacket showed off her slender waist, though the khaki color did nothing for her complexion. She slipped her shoes on. "The forest is beautiful this time of year," she mumbled over and over, as she readied herself. Rehearsal never hurt, even though she knew she could never speak the words aloud outside of their hotel room. At least, not until James Hamilton was standing in front of them.

~14~

"Weren't the royals wonderful?" Lynn gushed as she and Alfred unlocked the door to their Savoy suite. "And they truly understood the importance of the play." She unbuckled her jacket's belt and popped the buttons open. Tossing the jacket on a nearby chair, she headed for the bedroom.

"I saw the queen weeping," Alfred said, "though I'm not sure anyone else did. She was very discreet with her handkerchief." He followed his wife into the adjoining room.

"We've had floods of tears in the theater all over England. The message of the need for strength in times of chaos really helps bolster people," Lynn said. "Even the royal family, it seems." She flopped down on the bed without even taking her shoes off. "But I am exhausted."

"You were the hit of the afternoon, my dear," Alfred said. "They should make you a dame of the realm for all that you do." He hung up his hat and his jacket, took off his shoes and padded over to the bed.

"A dream I've always aspired to, Alfred." Lynn sighed. "But I don't see it happening anytime soon. Right now, the real heroes are the boys overseas, the ones laying down their lives for the rest of us. My time may come."

"If not, you will always be the dame of my realm." Alfred leaned over and planted a kiss on her forehead.

She pulled him down next to her. "You are my shining knight, Alfred. You were wonderful today, as usual." She waved a hand as he opened his mouth, undoubtedly to protest. "No, don't do this to yourself. You delivered those lines with such passion." She reached to pat him on the chest and collided with his arm coming to meet hers.

They dissolved into laughter.

Alfred said, "Remember the time I whacked you on the head when I thought you let the dog up on the bed? I thought I was shoving the pooch off. Your howl was a pretty good facsimile of hers."

"Your only saving grace was that it was the middle of the night, and so dark you couldn't see your hand in front of your face." In spite of herself, she smiled at the memory, more because of Alfred's horror, and his immediate over the top apologies.

The phone rang.

Alfred groaned.

"You just stay where you are, darling." Lynn sat up and turned enough to pat him on the chest, this time unimpeded. She swung her feet over the edge of the bed and headed for the telephone in the other room. "Hello. Lynn Fontanne here." What came through the wire was the familiar voice of their stage manager at the Aldwych. As Lynn listened, her face fell. "Just a moment, please. Alfred needs to hear this too." She went to the bedroom door and motioned Alfred over.

She was afraid he could read the look on her face. He sat up and pivoted, his fists supporting him on either side. He pushed himself off the bed and strode over to her.

Lynn stretched the phone cord so they could sit on the divan together. Alfred dropped down beside her as she positioned the receiver so they both could listen. He scrunched up his forehead and clamped his lips tight, sending a look of confusion to his wife.

"All right, Sam, go ahead," Lynn said, ignoring what she read as Alfred's silent question. "Alfred's right here with me, and we both can hear you."

Alfred leaned in so they were shoulder to shoulder, almost ear to ear.

"The theater was bombed this afternoon while you were at Windsor," Sam said, without preamble.

A long pause. Lynn felt Alfred's muscles tense, just as hers did. This could not be good news. "And?" she asked, before rushing on. "Was anyone hurt? What's the extent of the damage? Will we be able to play?" Alfred's touch on her knee brought the litany to a close.

Sam sighed on the other end of the line, boding ill news. "Yes, the theater is damaged some, but mostly the façade. The seats and the stage and those environs have minimal damage. Mostly things falling that need some repair. But..."

Lynn held her breath. That "but" sent a frisson of foreboding along her neck. She reached out and grasped Alfred's hand.

"But?" Alfred asked. "What else? Don't hesitate. We need to know the whole story."

The Lunts waited. Apparently, Sam was unwilling to break too abruptly into whatever the news was.

"Come, Sam," Lynn said, "tell us, please. Share whatever the burden may be. It's far better to know than to suffer in ignorance."

"There's no easy way to say this, because I know how close you both were to him." Another pause.

Were? Him?

Pip, Lynn mouthed to Alfred, who nodded in return. "It's Pip, isn't it? Please, what happened?"

Sam cleared his throat. "Yes. Pip was killed from the blast." He went on in a rush. "He was apparently right outside the theater, heading in to check the costumes, and whatever else needed doing, when the bomb hit. It was as if the theater was targeted directly. I–"

"What can we do to help?" Lynn asked. "Does he have family? Who should we contact?" She thought immediately of James Hamilton. He needed to be notified. Pip was the link between them, and, from the way Hamilton talked, a very important link. That coupled with–

She realized Alfred was speaking. She forced herself back into the scene on the divan.

"So, you've contacted...Who? Does his family know?" Alfred said.

"Yes, that's all being taken care of, even as we speak," Sam said. "But I wanted to call you personally. There's really not anything more we can do. At least, right now. Maybe later, for a funeral or memorial service. I'll keep you informed. Um..."

"I know what you want to say," Lynn said. "It seems terribly callous, but I'm sure you want to know if tonight's performance should be canceled." She nodded at Alfred.

"We think we should cancel," Alfred voiced her nod. "But can things be cleaned up for tomorrow? That feels rather heartless, but, considering the message of the play, and the need of our audiences for that catharsis, we probably shouldn't put off too long."

"Please don't think us heartless, Sam," Lynn said. "We are far from that." Sam made conciliatory noises. "I know Pip would want the run to continue. He was so enthusiastic about the play." She crossed her fingers and showed them to Alfred.

"I agree," Sam said, and Lynn uncrossed her fingers. "Pip raved about you two. And the play too, of course. I think he'd want us to open tomorrow. We have only an evening performance tomorrow, so we should have time to cart away the rubble. They're clearing the street right now, in fact."

"What time is blackout tomorrow? Seven o'clock, as usual? If so, we can begin the performance at our regular curtain time of six," Alfred said. "People can get to the theater before it's dark, and find their way home as usual after."

"That's right. I'll make sure everything is checked out, so there is no surprise of a weak ceiling or something. Right now, from what we know, the structure is fully intact," Sam said.

"Poor Pip," Lynn said, her voice thick with sorrow. "He was such a dear boy."

"All our condolences to the entire cast and crew," Alfred said. "We can do a short tribute before curtain tomorrow. We don't want him to simply fade away without some remembrance."

"I'll set something up," Sam said. "Leave it to me. I'm sure we can get some flowers, at least."

They thanked him, and, after a few simple exchanges about Hitler and Pip, they rang off.

Lynn returned to her earlier thread of thought about the significance of Pip. Even more so, about the message he wanted conveyed to James Hamilton. She turned to face Alfred and took a hold of both his hands. "The forest is beautiful this time of year."

Alfred's eyebrows went up and his mouth gaped a bit. "Oh, Lord, Lynnie, I think you're right."

He leaped right into her thoughts, jumping ahead to what she had not yet voiced. Now she did. "He might have been targeted, Alfred. Pip found out something, and they–whoever is Hitler's connection here–had him eliminated. They perhaps used the theater bombing as a coverup. Hopefully, they don't know about Pip's message for James through us."

"I don't think they do, Lynnie. Or we might have been attacked ourselves. But I'd bet they're watching us, to see which way we lean."

"I agree," Lynn said.

"But then, wouldn't it be obvious from the anti-war themes of the play?" Alfred said, but then corrected himself. "We are pretty closed-lipped in public about our feelings, though, so maybe they're just waiting to see which way the wind blows for us."

Lynn nodded. "I see where you're going with this, darling. If we can be manipulated, that would certainly be to their advantage. We are, after all, very well known, and could sway people to our side. Or their side, if they think they can influence us to go along with them."

"We could be a great help to James, if he agrees to use us in that manner," Alfred said. "We have the ability to 'become' anyone we wish. Perhaps we could become closet sympathizers. We're actors, after all."

"The best in the business," Lynn said.

Alfred put his arms around Lynn and drew her in. "Whatever it takes. Pip deserves our best efforts. Tomorrow night–"

Lynn finished the thought, "We take out the blue apron."

-15-

Lynn stood in her blue apron as Alfred's character exhorted his son to take the utmost care, and did he really want to join the war effort? The lines flowed out between the two, brought alive by superb acting. But Lynn could hardly keep her mind on the play. Without effort, she usually sank into the character she was portraying, having absorbed every last word, created every gesture and facial expression, to say nothing of body language, with such attention to detail that audiences saw not Lynn Fontanne, but the woman she was playing.

Tonight was different. The blue apron. Would James be there to see it? Or at least one of his compatriots? Lynn forced her mind to occupy the set, and not mentally reiterate the lines Pip gave them: "The forest is beautiful this time of year." She had no idea what that meant, but it was clearly of some import. There was no chance of her forgetting the line. Heaven knew, she could retrieve lines from a play they were in years before. But still, she worried.

She knew she could channel her own concern and nervousness into her character, so no one in the audience would suspect the reason for her unrest. The last act was the worst, with half her mind heading for the dressing room where, with luck on their side, Hamilton's aide, or perhaps the man himself, would appear to help assuage their burden.

Finally, the curtain lowered. Lynn woke up to the sniffles and weeping in the audience, the usual catharsis making itself known as the lights came up. She fervently hoped for a shorter number of curtain calls, but it was not to be. Twelve tonight.

After accolades from patrons greeting them backstage, Lynn clutched Alfred's sleeve, pulling him close. "I will burst, if I must see anyone else. Please, darling..." She knew he would read her eyes.

"Of course," he whispered. He turned to the others. "Miss Fontanne is simply exhausted from tonight's performance. That, and she's probably famished. I know I am. Please accept our excuses, and we'll retire to our dressing room."

The stage manager cringed. "There is just one more couple clamoring for your blessing. Just to touch the hem of your garments." He cocked his head and smiled.

Lynn appeared to relent. "Oh, all right. If that couple wants to greet us in our dressing room, do allow that. We know these people are living through hell. They deserve a bit of a respite."

"But perhaps only those two tonight, please. We really are frazzled." Alfred slipped her hand through his crooked elbow and led her off. "Just give us a few minutes to get out of these costumes," he called back over his shoulder.

The door to the dressing room closed firmly behind them, Lynn took off the blue apron and held it up before her. "You've done your job, my pretty. Now it's time to do ours." She hung it on the coat rack and dropped down on the stool in front of her makeup mirror. "I hope somebody comes looking for that blue apron."

Alfred, his costume already tossed over the screen in the corner, grabbed his dressing gown. "We can only hope, Lynnie." He maneuvered his arms into the sleeves and reached for the tasseled belt, pulling it tight. He plopped down without fanfare into a nearby easy chair and levered his shoes off.

A knock on the door.

Lynn blew a stray hair off her forehead. "Well, here they come." She shuffled her shoulders and, with a forced relaxed sigh, called, "Come in!"

The door swung open and an oversized bouquet of flowers appeared, with tweed pants and leather shoes below. James Hamilton's face peeked around the blooms. "Yes, dear, they're here!"

Lynn recognized the tones of...well, melodrama, perhaps. He was portraying a starstruck fan, apparently. She couldn't help grinning. "Welcome."

"I'm James Hamilton. And here's my lovely wife, Heather." He clearly didn't want anyone made aware that they'd met before. "The performance was, well, simply astounding!" He gushed a few more praises as he thrust the bouquet at Lynn, urged his wife forward into the room with a hand at her back, and simultaneously seemed to trip a bit, causing his foot to catch on the door and slam it shut.

Heather, taller than her husband, sported a cloud of blond curls framing her long face. Her face lit up as she spotted Lynn and Alfred, clearly smitten.

"Well done!" James patted his hands together in silent applause. "Quite a performance!"

Lynn went to the door, cracked it open a bit to reveal a crew member standing guard. "Please dismiss anyone else with my profound apologies. We really do need to get back for some rest." She sent out a brilliant smile, belied by eyes that drooped with fatigue. She shut the door and leaned against it, as if to prevent any intruders from assailing their lair. "And now?..."

James and Heather dropped all pretense of people overcome with awe at the Lunts' presence. "May we sit?" James asked.

Alfred drew chairs closer and motioned for them to take a seat. "Please."

Lynn vibrated with pent up questions. "Did you see–" She stopped herself. Her voice took on a lilt of nonchalance. "Don't you just love our dressing room? It makes me feel so...so, safe." She mimed a microphone, with a fist close to her mouth, and the other hand cupped behind her ear.

"Your people have been closely vetted," Heather said, "and no one has been in here since you went out for the last act. Plus, we have our own guard posted, so it is safe."

"To answer your question," James said, "yes, we saw the blue apron. What have you found?"

"Not what we've found," Alfred said, "but rather a message for you from Pip."

There was an uncomfortable silence.

Heather dropped her chin and fiddled with the catch on her purse.

James closed his eyes and nodded. "We heard about his death. We are so very sorry." He folded his hands in his lap and leaned forward.

"Was he targeted?" Alfred asked.

"Very likely," James answered. "Nothing we can prove for sure. But the fact that he passed along a message, points in that direction."

"The message. Yes," Lynn said. "He said to tell you, the forest is beautiful this time of year."

Hamilton's brow furrowed deeply enough for sowing. His eyes narrowed and he ran his hand up and across his chin. "Forest."

"The forest is beautiful," Heather said. "Beautiful forest."

The pair exchanged a glance so full of meaning, even Lynn could read it.

"That means something, doesn't it," Lynn said. "What does it tell you?"

"It tells us that Pip discovered the Nazi sympathizer. We narrowed it down to a few men, but couldn't seem to get any further. How he did, I'll never know, but I'm not willing to dispute his findings. He was a tenacious agent, one who explored every crack and crevice."

"He was that kind of worker here too," Alfred said. "Meticulous and organized."

Lynn was losing patience. "So, what does it mean? You seem to be fixed on the beautiful forest part, rather than this time of year."

James sat back in the chair, his hands gripping the armrests. "We don't want to put you in danger. The less you know, the safer you'll probably be."

Alfred scoffed. "I've never known that to be true. We need every scrap of information you have, so as not to slip up with anyone. Loose lips may sink ships, but loose minds will surely lose a war."

Lynn leaned forward. "You must tell us. There has to be a way we can help. We don't want Pip to have died, only to put all of us in mortal danger that we may not even be aware of."

James tented his fingers in front of his mouth. He sighed, and exchanged a look of painful acquiescence with his wife. She nodded. "Heather doesn't often have anything to do with my work, but I've briefed her on Pip's mission, just so she doesn't slip up. I suppose you two deserve the same. You realize, of course, that what I am about to tell you is top secret. You know we've been trying to expose a Nazi sympathizer here in England?"

Lynn and Alfred both nodded.

"He's more than simply a sympathizer. This man has power and money, and is more than willing to spend it to see England destroyed and brought under Hitler's command. He never slips up when he's here in London. But we know he is in direct communication somehow with the high powers in Germany. We feel there's a plan...some kind of plan...being developed, but we don't know what they're planning. Aerial attacks with a new kind of weapon? U-boats in the Channel? Landings?" He raised his hands, palms up and blew out a breath that reeked of exasperation. "But it's crucial we find out."

"What does that have to do with Pip's message of a forest?" Lynn asked.

"A beautiful forest," Heather said.

James nodded. "This is a bit of a long-winded explanation, but I'm sure this is what he was trying to tell us. Centuries ago, 1066, to be exact, the Normans invaded England." He held up a hand to forestall a comment forming on Alfred's lips. "Hear me out. It does all connect."

Alfred settled back into his seat and clasped his hands in his lap.

"Anyway," Hamilton continued, "land was given to the lords who helped William the Conqueror. One of those lords received a nice parcel in Kent, with a view of, and access to, the Channel. His name was Beauforêt."

"Beauforêt!" Lynn whispered. "Beautiful forest." She frowned. "But I've never heard of an English lord with that name."

James shook his head. "No, of course not. Because over the years, it was Anglicized, if you will. The original Beauforêt turned into Bufort, the 'boe' becoming 'bue', and the 'forêt' corrupted into 'fort' or 'furt' depending on the speed of the speaker."

"Lord Bufort." Lynn laid a finger on her lips. "Now, I have heard of him. A man who loves to party."

"More to the point," James said, "a man who loves the theater. A man who loves to entertain."

"Wait just a moment," Lynn flapped a hand in Alfred's direction. "The roses. That bouquet on my dressing table." She swiveled her hand to point a perfectly manicured index finger to a vase of red and pink roses. "Check the card, Alfred. I'm sure–"

But Alfred was already ahead of her. He held the small card aloft. "Yes, indeed, Lynnie. From Alain Bufort." He handed the card off to Hamilton. "This isn't the first time, either, if I recall."

"You're right, Alfred, once or twice before, I think. I didn't recognize the name, as I really don't for many of our admirers, but I did take notice of more than one accolade like this over the past couple of months."

"Not every night, of course," Alfred said. "This one came, what? Two nights ago?"

Lynn confirmed that with a nod. "Those bouquets stand out because we rarely get more than one from the same admirer."

"He clearly loves the theater," Alfred said. "Well, at least our play and our performance."

"I'm surprised he hasn't approached you to visit his estate in Kent," Heather said. "He does love to show off celebrities."

Lynn's brain flashed to a scene in a manor house, a man and a woman lifting a flute of champagne, laughing, sharing inane conversation. She could do inane conversation if needed. She could also be bright, witty, intelligent, devil-may-care... Her thoughts were interrupted.

"Lynnie." Alfred's voice came through. "I know that look. What are you concocting?"

As if he didn't know. Lynn knew her husband through and through. He was providing an opening into a scheme he would wholeheartedly support, she suspected.

She sent him a smile that she knew would corroborate his own thoughts. "Lord Bufort loves to entertain." It was not even close to a question. "He loves the theater, and he loves us." She turned to James. "He's been here to see us. He's seen our play. But has he met us yet?" She knew he had not. Once introduced, she remembered everyone who graced her with their presence.

James shook his head. "No, you said as much. And no to your next proposal. It's far too dangerous."

The man was too astute. Lynn relaxed into what she hoped looked like acceptance. But she caught sight of Heather, who had a hand to her mouth, concealing, no doubt, a knowing smile. Heather's eyes gave her away, though she didn't say a word. *Well, at least I've got her on my side*, Lynn thought. She allowed one side of her mouth to curve upward a bit as her gaze shifted back to James. "Well, I know this is an audacious proposal, but shouldn't we at least meet the man, make ourselves accessible, perhaps even provide some light entertainment for one of his soirées? You said he loves to flaunt his connections with celebrities."

"That is a most wonderful idea, Lynnie," Alfred said, as Lynn knew he would. "We could distract him a bit from his machinations with the Germans. Wouldn't that buy you some time to find out more about what he and his German partners are scheming?" He answered his own question without giving James a moment to squeak in. "Of course it would." He leaned forward and squeezed James's arm. "Let us help."

James's head stopped bobbling back and forth in an unspoken no. "Far too dangerous. How could we ever extract you if you end up down in Kent, instead of here in London, where we have much more control? When he's in London, he is unimpeachable. No suspicious moves, no contact with anyone known to be a sympathizer. Nothing. We do watch his movements, of course, but he's given us nothing." He clasped his hands in his lap, fingertips turning white as he gripped. "On his Kent estate, however, that's a different story. We think. There are people coming and going, guests mostly, not many locals, but once inside...Pfff." He opened his hands and held them palms up. "They disappear. We have not been able to get even close. The manor house is set way back from the road, and is heavily policed. We've tried, considering we can't see much of his security force. But we found out early on that there's no way in."

"But we can get in," Alfred said. "If he loves the theater here in London, and us in particular, maybe we can wangle an invitation to visit his estate."

"It's possible he'll approach you. He's been at your play often enough. We're fairly sure he's one to watch." Tenting his hands in front of his mouth, James frowned and shook his head. "But it would be impossible to protect or extract you from the estate in Kent."

Silence reigned.

Lynn watched Hamilton with a hawk's eye. Alfred seemed to get the message too, as he stood with arms folded and waiting. Lynn thought she saw cracks in the armor of Hamilton's resolve not to put them in danger, not to get them too deeply involved. She went to him and crouched down, placing her hands on his. "We are powerful people, James. We can become what you need us to become. We do this every night on the stage. Let us help. For Pip's sake, let us help. For England's sake, and the Allies. Please, James. Please."

Lynn watched as Hamilton's face went from rigid tight lips to eyes raised to heaven. He was weakening.

James blew out a deep breath through his nose. "He's given us nothing here in London. He's far too careful. Maybe down in Kent..." Capitulation. "We must be meticulous in our planning," he said, sending glances to Lynn and Alfred that were filled with sparks and warnings.

Lynn recognized a win.

~16~

They had to wait a few weeks before another floral tribute arrived, this time delivered before the performance.

"I know what this means," Alfred said. "He's getting ready to approach us in person. Do you think we should acknowledge him during one of the curtain calls?"

"That's not a bad idea, Alfred. A little sweep of an arm, a simple curtsy–"

"I am *not* curtsying, Lynnie," Alfred broke in. "I don't care if he is a lord."

Lynn giggled. "That's one of my favorite things about you, Alfred."

"What, darling? My impeccable curtsy?"

With a playful sideways look, she cuffed him on the arm. "Yes, that too. But more your quick wit."

"The only way to match yours, my dear."

Lynn turned serious. "Find out where he's seated. My money is on the closest box, the one we've had an eye on. That will be easy enough to doff our hats to."

"Done and done." Alfred set off to finalize their plans.

Backstage after the performance was a maelstrom of activity. The Lunts left their dressing room door open, and spent an hour accepting the paeans of their fans. Finally, the torrent weakened to a trickle. Lynn pulled her mouth to one side and frowned a miniscule frown. She wondered if they missed their cue with Lord Bufort. Alfred began pacing. Neither said a word.

The trickle of fans stopped and...nothing.

When the man built like a fire hydrant appeared in the doorway, they were unprepared for his appearance. "That was the most magnificent performance yet. I've seen it four times now, and each time is a little different. But tonight's is surely my favorite." He swept into the room. Or, as Lynn thought, more like rolled into the room. The man grasped Alfred's hand in both of his. "I should really introduce myself. I'm Lord Bufort, Lord Alain Bufort." He pumped Alfred's hand. "Bloody impolite of me not to tell you right away. But I'm just swept away with the two of you."

"Alfred Lunt," Alfred said. It seemed more to get a word in edgewise than announce his well-known name.

"We're delighted to meet you, Lord Bufort." Lynn's welcome pulled the lord's attention to her. "And thank you for the wonderfully fragrant flower bouquets you sent us before as well." Nothing like laying it on rather thick to show they noticed his attentions.

"Oh, Alain, please." He turned back to Alfred. "All my friends call me Alain."

"Alfred will suffice here as well." Alfred was putting on his best hale, fellow, well met persona.

"Delighted," Bufort said. "Miss Fontanne, you were wonderful."

Lynn smiled and lowered her gaze. No "Call me Lynn." No, she was setting up her character. "Thank you." Her voice was demure, her eyebrows were lifted just enough to indicate delicate surprise. *My breakout role way back in 1919 is serving me well now,* she thought. *That ditzy Dulcy becomes the slightly ditzy Lynn, rather than the sophisticated woman most people see me as. I hope Lord Bufort buys it.*

Apparently, he was buying it. He clapped his hands, then lifted them to his mouth, gasping a bit. "I have a most wonderful idea! I could barely wait to tell you. You must come down to my manor house in Kent as my guests. Perhaps you might consider gracing us with a reading or two? Forest Hall will be just the place for some fun."

Forest Hall. Beautiful Forest, Lynn thought. *Oh, Pip!*

"Please say yes!" Bufort's face was turning a high shade of rose.

Who in heaven's name would think this little fop was colluding with the Germans? Lynn caught herself. *Of course, that's just the person he would want to appear as, isn't it?*

Alfred had a quizzical look on his face. "Did you hear me, Lynnie? What do you think? We do have some days off next week. Should we go?"

"What?" Stay in character, Lynn. But she didn't want to slather it on too heavily. That would be hard to maintain for a long period of time, if it weren't on stage. "Oh, yes, Alfred. I think we should take advantage of Lord Bufort's offer. I'd love to get out of London for a bit."

Alfred turned to Bufort. "It's settled then. If we can come down on Monday, which is a day the theater is dark anyway, we could spend several days with you. We do have to be back for a Friday evening performance."

"Perfect," Bufort said. "Stay as long as you wish. It's an idyllic setting. A good place to remove yourselves for a bit from the terrors of London." He reached out to shake hands with both of them. "My steward will be in touch tomorrow to finalize all the details. For now, I really should leave you two to rest. You must be exhausted. We'll work out everything tomorrow." He turned to go, but stopped in the doorway. "Please pick something light to do a reading for us. I fear that we are all so weary of the ongoing attacks and the war that we would appreciate something less...oppressive, shall we say?" He left, closing the door behind him, without waiting for an answer.

Alfred exchanged a triumphant look with Lynn. "We'll find readings that–"

"Play right into his leanings," Lynn finished. She went to Alfred and reached up to plant a kiss on his cheek.

Hamilton was contacted and a meeting set up with Lynn and Alfred at the Savoy. They came back from the theater, driven through dark streets in a car with shaded headlights and little else to guide their way. The same as many nights before.

James was waiting for them in their suite. No surprise that he was able to enter like a wraith, perhaps even walk through walls. Lynn chuckled as she greeted him.

Within several hours, she was no longer chuckling. He filled them both with information about Lord Bufort's history, his involvement in fringe groups at school, his fear of communism. And finally, his apparent belief that Nazis could save the world. Apparent, because he refused to discuss politics in public, having gone almost underground in that respect. But enough information leaked out to add his name to the list of those suspected of collusion, or at least a bit too frequent communication, with the Reich.

By three in the morning, Lynn and Alfred were filled to the brim with Hamilton's briefings, as well as with too many cups of strong coffee.

"One more thing," James said, standing up to stretch and shake out his hands.

Lynn tried not to groan audibly. Foolish, as she and Alfred often drove themselves to distraction working on perfecting their roles. Complaining was not often in their vocabulary. And certainly shouldn't be, in this hour of England's direst need. She drew herself up. "Anything you wish, James. We are at your service."

Hamilton dug in his pocket and produced what resembled a small cigarette lighter.

"Ah! Compliments of...you?" Alfred said.

"No," James said. "Compliments of the British government. It's a Minox mini-camera." He handed it off to Alfred.

Alfred turned it over and over, checking it out. "No. I don't believe it."

"Believe it. It's smaller than most lighters, so don't let anybody get too close. Best to keep it hidden either way," James said, retrieving the camera from Alfred. "Watch." He proceeded to demonstrate how the miniature camouflaged camera worked, then handed it back to Alfred to try his hand.

Alfred mastered the movements, repeating them a dozen times, just as he rehearsed for the theater. "I think I've got it. This is a marvel."

"Anything you can find to photograph would help us immensely. But–" James waggled a finger at both of them, adding a firm look of warning to go with it. "Do not put yourself in danger to do it. And don't let it fall into someone else's hands."

Lynn looked up from her own practice with the camera. "We will do our very best, James."

Hamilton picked up his coat, slung it across his shoulders and headed for the door. He paused and took a deep breath. "I've crammed you with as much as I could in this short time. I hope to God it's enough."

"I'm sure you've done your best, James," Lynn said. "Now, it's time for us to do ours." She dared not say more, knowing that they were going into the lion's den without knowing if they did indeed have enough.

James sent them a salute. "Come home safe, you two. We'll be watching you as close as we can."

Alfred saw him out and turned back to Lynn, his face serious. "I hope we can do this, Lynnie."

"This is our most important role, darling," she said. "I know we can do this. We must."

-17-

The Lunts managed to exit London with minimal fanfare. Now, they stood on the platform outside a tiny train station in Kent, waiting for Lord Bufort's promised car. The stationmaster rang up the lord, as instructed, and the message delivered that a car was on its way, give or take an hour or so.

Bufort wanted to shepherd them from London in his car, but the Lunts insisted on the train. Troops were on the move all the time, and they themselves could get to Forest Hall on the coast without too much trouble. It took a bit of persuasion, but they reminded the lord that they always traveled by train. It gave them time to decompress. And time to prepare themselves for a new scene to play. Besides, the trains getting them from New York to Ten Chimneys, their summer estate back in the States, were negotiated with little problem. They assured Lord Bufort that indulging in soaking up the English scenery along the way would give them great pleasure as well, not having been in Kent before. They prevailed.

Lynn, usually the paragon of patience, was shifting her feet and wiggling her shoulders. "It's getting a bit nippy," she said, sidling up to Alfred. He put his arm around her and pulled her coat collar up against her neck.

She wanted to wear her uniform to Forest Hall, but Alfred nixed that. "Bufort will take offense, considering we're entering his territory, and we're pretty sure we know how he feels about the Allies. I think he'd miss the irony of the uniforms."

She capitulated. "Alfred, we must remember to call him Lord Bufort. I think he's the type that, no matter what he says, he relishes the title and the adulation it probably brings him. Especially if he's trying to hide his true feelings about things."

"Nope," Alfred said. "No Lord for me. He said to call him Alain, and that's what it'll be. I'm a hale-fellow-well-met American, remember. We don't kowtow to anybody."

"Except General Eisenhower..." She smiled sweetly. "And me, of course."

That sent Alfred into hearty laughter.

Just then, they heard the rumble of a car, and a Bentley came cruising around the corner and up to the station.

"My goodness," Lynn whispered to Alfred, "how does he maintain that dragon, what with gas rationing and all."

"People like him have ways," Alfred whispered back, before striding down the steps to greet the chauffeur.

Lynn affected a miniscule slouch, topped with a pretty pout. "At last!" she called out. "The dampness is creeping right up my stockings." She hoped that wasn't too much. It didn't appear to be, as the man seemed busy only with opening the boot and storing their luggage. Although she was tempted to hitch up her skirt just a bit, she resisted. Too much would be just a bit...too much.

The car was warm and Lynn relaxed as best she could into the plush upholstery. "Almost as good as a Rolls, right, Alfred?" Said just loud enough for the driver, who stiffened at the words.

She checked her watch. Fifty-three minutes along, the driver turned off, cruising between two monoliths and past opened gates. The gravel road seemed reasonably maintained, and Lynn spent her time craning to see past the driver and out the front windshield, a rather fruitless venture.

As if the road felt her frustration rising, the drive swept to the left, affording a view of the manor house itself off to the right, aglow in the afternoon sunlight.

"Look, Alfred! I believe we've arrived!" Lynn pointed at the house sitting on a spacious lawn. "Quite imposing, isn't it?"

The driver slowed. "The view is always worth the wait."

The house was a solid rectangle of pale stone, three stories tall, with chunky chimneys marching hither and yon across the roof. The front was faced with windows, like eyes looking out on the landing strip of gravel that curved gently from the right toward a front portico before launching forward and disappearing into a wooded area well beyond the end of the house. Somewhere, that lane must lead to outbuildings: a garage, a stable, perhaps a caretaker's cottage.

The driver accelerated. As the car moved into a grove of trees, the road bent right, and the house disappeared from view.

"Oh-h-h!" Lynn drew out a disappointed response.

"Not to worry, ma'am," the driver said. "We'll come out soon enough."

The road cruised down a soft slope before emerging from the woods and curving left again. The house sprang into view. They were almost on it, affording a dramatic presentation.

"Look! There's a wing shooting off toward the back garden," Lynn said.

The driver chuckled. "From that first view before the grove, you couldn't see the whole house, only the main part. There are wings going back off each end, built out toward the sea. Can't see the water from here either, though, but it's out there."

"Looks like we're in for a treat, Lynnie," Alfred said. "Pretty impressive, even what we can see."

The driver took up his tale. "It's a lovely estate. Bit smaller than when ol' Conqueror Willie gave it to 'em."

"Dates back to the Norman conquest, then," Alfred said.

"Yessir. Those wings were added later, though. Lots of changes over the time the Buforts have been here."

"Original owners, then?" Alfred asked.

The driver nodded. They drew up in front of the main entrance.

As grand manor houses went, the portico was not terribly imposing, but rather, harmonious to the size of the house. Probably not original, Lynn thought, and the windows must have been added in the Elizabethan era, when glass was more affordable, and light as well as pleasant views in country houses was cherished. But she didn't share her ideas, the better to adhere to her role as a sparkling wit, not an intellectual.

Above a set of wide and curving steps, just enough to remind the visitor that the owner here was up a level from the rest of the world, the great double doors stood heavy and dark within the portico. The doors were riotous with carved figures around two very large doorknockers, one on each door. Surmounting the doors was a piedmont porch extending out enough to shield arriving guests from blustery weather. Two plain pillars in the front supported the porch roof. The light stone served to emphasize the imposing doors, enough to straighten one's spine into at least a semblance of respect for the honorable owners of such a grand manor house. Mammoth flower urns filled to overflowing with all sorts of greenery and early blooming plants softened the entry.

Lynn was delighted. The weather was breezy, but warm, on this late April morning, belying T.S. Eliot's claim that April was the cruelest month. "Lord Bufort must have a greenhouse to have flowers so early in the season." She was trolling for information.

The driver turned in his seat to answer. "Yes, ma'am. And a lovely place it is, too." He waved a hand off to the right of the house. "Back there hidden away."

"Stunning," Lynn said.

One of the manor house doors opened, slow and ponderous, and Lord Bufort stepped out. His face broke out in a wide grin and he bounced down the steps, like an overblown soccer ball headed for the pitch, and swept open the Bentley's door to release Lynn and Alfred.

"Welcome, welcome, welcome!" he boomed. "Forest Hall awaits your pleasure."

Lynn grasped his outstretched hand and emerged from the car. Alfred was right behind. "Oh, Lord Bufort–"

"Alain, please. Alain," the lord said. "We don't stand on ceremony with visitors much here." He tucked Lynn's hand into the crook of his elbow. "Don't worry about the luggage. The help will bring it up. Come in, come in!" He kept up a running commentary as he led the Lunts up the steps to the door.

Lynn, ever observant, caught the driver maneuvering the car down the lane past the building. She stopped just under the portico and turned to Alain. "Do you have stables back there, somewhere?" She flapped her hand off toward where the car disappeared.

"Part of the stables was converted to garages when cars came into fashion, but yes, we do have a couple of horses. Do you ride?"

"Enthusiastically!" Lynn said. "I hope we can do that one of the days we're here?"

The query brought a smile to Alain's lips. "Of course. Once you are settled and I have shown you around. Perhaps tomorrow. We'll watch the weather. We're right on the coast, so we've learned to keep an eye out."

"Splendid," Lynn said. "Are there more guests coming? I so hope so, don't you, Alfred?" She craned around to send him a rather vacuous smile.

Alain led them under the portico. "The others arrive tomorrow. Two couples more local to the area were invited, and four gentlemen, business acquaintances, will join us sometime tomorrow also. But for now, let's in to tea."

Lynn tucked the information away. One never knew when something would be useful. Especially here. Especially now. This was not a stage set, not a frivolous romantic comedy, not even a drama that would wrap up nice and tidy in a couple of hours. She must be on guard and put all of her considerable talents to use. She smiled up at Alain and squeezed his arm. "I can't wait." She turned to her husband, trailing along behind them. "I know you can't either, Alfred."

"Truly said, Lynnie."

They stepped into the house and a servant closed the door behind them.

The heavy thud came close to making Lynn flinch. Dante must have felt about the same upon entering the gates of Hell. To forestall a shiver, she lifted her chin and said, in a deliberate light tone. "I hope the tea is Earl Grey."

-18-

The next morning, the Earl Grey, along with a full hot breakfast, was waiting for them. Lord Bufort was already at the table, ready to tackle a full plate of piping hot eggs and toast. The cook, he told the Lunts, prepared daily meals and then returned home. "I like to begin my morning quite alone," Alain said. "Everyone knows I crave solitude at breakfast. Of course, there's a small staff here now, what with the war. We make do."

At that, the butler faded away into the kitchen, clearly attuned to his employer's preferences.

"Perhaps we should take breakfast in our room," Lynn said. "We certainly don't want to impose on you."

"Not at all, not at all. You are quite welcome company at my table. I am honored," Bufort assured them.

The conversation at the table started out light and frothy. Deliberate, it seemed to Lynn, perhaps to keep them placated and off their guard. Of course, Lord Bufort–Alain, she amended–had no reason to suspect them of espionage. They were here because he was enamored of the theater, and probably even more so of Lynn and Alfred. Though just the three of them were at the breakfast table, Alain assured them that yes, the other guests would arrive later in the day, providing them with a small, but intimate, audience for their reading, scheduled for Wednesday evening.

Lynn picked up a scone, split it, and slathered it with clotted cream. The fragrance of rashers wafted across the room as Alfred raised the lid on the silver chafing dish. Her stomach growled.

Alain lifted his head from the sugar tongs he was wielding, and sent her a raised eyebrow. "Apparently, we haven't fed you enough."

Lynn puffed out an airy giggle. "So sorry! I'm always hungry in the morning. Ask Alfred."

Alfred took up the gauntlet. "Eats like a horse at breakfast. Especially if she's been outside traipsing around the garden, cutting flowers."

Never in her life did she cut her own flowers. There were always teenage boys from the village to hire for the cutting part, while she carried the basket. Alfred was the gardener. But this tiny exchange gave her another piece to her character. Who knew where it might lead? "Truly, Alfred's the farming expert, not I." She held a hand up to her mouth, then whispered through her fingers. "But I do love the flowers."

"Thank you, darling." Alfred joined her at the table, choosing the spot next to her.

"You're in luck, then," Alain said, lifting the teapot to offer Lynn a refill, which she gratefully accepted. "The greenhouse is stuffed with flowers this time of year. Our gardener insists on caring for them like his children. Overwintering, seeding at the proper time, potting things up in preparation for transplanting outdoors."

"Oh, how wonderful," Lynn trilled. "Do you have a green thumb yourself?"

Alain shook his head. "Not at all. Besides, all of that is too menial for me. No interest, no talent."

Lynn felt Alfred's foot nudge hers. *Pay attention*, it said.

"I can't bear to think of gardening right now," Alfred said. "If I can't get my hands in the good dirt at our estate, I'm better off keeping my mind off it."

Lynn picked up. "Speaking of estate, I'm really looking forward to the tour of the grounds you promised us last night. Can we do that this morning, please?"

"Right after breakfast," Alain said. "Though it's not like the major estates. The Normans were kind to our ancestor by bestowing this land, but it never was an estate in the old sense of the word. No village, no vicar, as the saying goes. We were endowed with plenty of land for our needs, but then, needs in 1066 were not quite as far ranging as a century or two later. So, even a century or two later, they had sheep, cattle, and enough room to grow what would feed the animals and them. What they didn't use, they could barter for what they couldn't grow or make."

"Didn't you ever lose any of it?" Lynn asked, hoping it sounded a bit nosey without being too offensive.

"Some. They left us with the cliffs." Alain picked up his cup and sat a moment, looking off toward the far end of the room.

Lynn knew he was remembering, unfocused, and maybe even a bit dejected at the loss. To put him off, she turned to follow his gaze, as if a painting or a person was taking his attention away. She pressed her luck. "Who took it away? Or was it some war?" She turned to load her fork with egg.

"Hmm. Well, we did reward our tenant farmer with a low price on his cottage and a bit of acreage when...I think it was my great-great-grandfather decided that he didn't want the trouble of animal husbandry..." Alain's voice trailed off, and Lynn noticed the distracted look again.

"Are you all right?" she asked. Might as well be blatant. That approach could become useful again sometime.

"Oh, Lynnie, leave the poor man alone. He's obviously got a lot on his mind." Alfred's voice had an edge of condescension. Lynn looked down at her plate.

"It's fine, Alfred," Alain said. "It's just that this war... Well, I had to fight a bit to keep the RAF from requisitioning what's left of my land. We're lucky that there's not enough here that would provide room for a landing...area. For the planes, you know."

A heartbeat of hesitation. Why? "Planes?" she asked. "You can't say they were going to put an airport on your land! Take away your land?" She was walking a fine edge, and she knew it. She leaned her leg into Alfred's.

Alain pushed his empty plate away and folded his hands. "Yes, it appears so."

Lynn sat silent, ruing a bit that Hamilton didn't give them much information on troop movements or plans. "How...strange," she said. She hoped it sounded as if she were about to say "unfortunate." That would be far too blunt, of course.

"We managed to fend them off," Alain said. "Between the weather and the lay of the land..." He shrugged. "Good luck for us."

Lynn folded her napkin and set it next to her fork. "Will your wife be joining us on our walk around the estate?" She sat up straight and sent a smile to Lord Bufort. *Let's see where he goes with this.*

"Unfortunately, no. She is with an elderly relative in Paris. Or rather, just outside of Paris," Alain said, throwing his own napkin onto his discarded plate.

"We just love Paris. Don't we, Alfred?" Lynn gushed, then reminded herself to dial back a bit. "Has she been there this whole time?" She would leave him to define "whole time."

"Since...back in 1940," Alain said, frowning. "I miss her terribly. But she insisted on staying to help out her aunt."

1940. The year the Germans...entered...Paris. Yes, there was Alfred's nudge again. They both caught that implication.

Alain pushed back his chair and stood, setting his hands on the table and leaning into them. "Shall we make the Grand Tour?"

Dismissal. Time to move onto more frivolous-and safer- topics.

"Delighted," Alfred said. He rose and held out a hand to Lynn, who joined him.

"Let's go out the French doors here." Alain gestured to the doors leading to a side terrace.

Once outside, Lynn oriented herself, and she could tell Alfred was doing the same. They stood on the terrace outside the dining room, which was on the ground floor of the north wing. She remembered from Alain's house tour of the day before that the north wing stretched east toward the sea from the left end of the Old Manor, as Alain called the main part of the house.

The Old Manor, with its central door where they arrived, was a study in symmetry. Once inside, the foyer contained a grand staircase that spiraled up through all three floors, ending in a lovely coffered ceiling high above them. To the right was a drawing room stretching along the front of the house, with a ceiling befitting a cathedral. Lynn could imagine blazing fires in the two massive fireplaces, and could almost hear the clink of armor and drinking cups. The room was old and filled with the most ancient furnishings and tapestries of the house.

After a circuit of the drawing room, admiring the paintings crowding the walls, the wall sconces dripping with crystal prisms, the mishmash of furniture styles, and the incongruous presence of armor tucked here and there, Alain led them back into the foyer.

"That reminds me of our house," Alfred said. "Nothing matches."

"If you love something, you should just bring it home," Lynn said.

Alain laughed. "When a house is as old as ours, then every ancestor certainly seized on that advice as well. Feels more lived in by real people."

They moved into the hallway leading deeper into the house, back past the drawing room, into one of the two wings making the Old Manor into a giant squared-off C, stretched out on its side.

The hallway was awash in sunlight, thanks to the bank of windows along the entire wall looking out into the back courtyard.

Lynn gasped in delight. "This is wonderful!"

"Quite," Alain said. "When the family added this wing to the Old Manor, that same great-great-somebody insisted on windows to bring in light. The other wing was built much earlier, of course, when one room led directly into another." He chopped the air to demonstrate. "Foyer to library to dining room, to what are now the kitchen rooms. This wing, however, has a corridor along one side. Makes for much more privacy. Quieter too."

Good to know, Lynn thought. Quiet could be very useful.

Alain led them on. Behind the drawing room was the lord's study. "I find this the most interesting room in the house. Originally, it was part of the drawing room, and there was a connecting door." Alain opened the hall door hardly more than a sliver, enough to gesture to the wall abutting the drawing room, now floor to ceiling bookcases protected behind mullioned glass. "One of my great-grandmothers–or maybe it was great-great. Either way, the woman of the house decided she wanted a private sitting room, so this room was carved out of part of the drawing room, and the door walled off on both sides. That wasn't enough, apparently, so the builders also took part of the buttery–the next room along–where the liquor, beer, and some of their food was stored. Sent the butler into apoplexy, I understand. He had to cram all of the various glasses, as well as the bottles and everything else, into what was left of a much larger storage area. No direct way into the drawing room either, where the men awaited their whiskeys. Did give the women a chance to get their sherry sooner, though."

Alain closed the door. "My grandfather turned it into his office, and so I keep it as such, my private study."

Lynn caught the word private. Interesting. Now her attention was piqued. A place certain to contain sensitive papers.

Alain opened the next door with a flourish, revealing a very modern addition: a toilet and bathing room.

Lynn walked in and peered into the adjoining bathing room. "Look at that enormous bathtub!"

"A tub fit for your former President Taft. From what I heard, he got stuck in his own bathtub in the White House."

They all chuckled.

"How up to date your ancestors were," Alfred said.

Lord Bufort laughed. "Not too far back, I'm afraid. This was added around 1870 sometime. Not so modern." They returned to the hall. He wagged a hand at two closed doors they passed. "The first room is what's left of the buttery, though it's used for storing just spirits now, and the glasses for serving them. No food. This second room is still used for what's needed to keep the conservatory healthy. The gardener fought heartily for that, I heard."

They reached the end of the corridor. Beyond was a pair of leaded glass French doors and sidelights. Lynn spotted a dazzling conservatory clothed in glass panels, diamonds and squares along all the walls as far as she could see. The perfect place to come in the winter, to soak up the meager English sun.

Alain opened the set of leaded glass French doors and ushered them down a short waterfall of steps into the conservatory. "Our gardener keeps up with botanical fashion. Not as much greenery as in earlier times, but a lovely spot anyway."

Lynn was enchanted. Wrought iron tables and chairs, plump cushions included, proffered an invitation to bide a while. She sighed and looked up to admire the pyramid of glass that topped the jewelbox of the room. Every paned wall sparkled in the morning sunlight. "A book, a spot of tea, and maybe even a sunhat." She giggled like a coquette. "What a wonderful hideaway."

Alain smiled and took her elbow. "Come. We'll go out onto the terrace." He opened the door at the side of the conservatory and they strolled out onto the courtyard terrace. Alain turned and explained the layout of the upper floors of the south wing they just traversed.

The first floor up was the master's bedroom and dressing room, the mistress's boudoir and suite, as well as a number of bedrooms, sitting rooms and salons for the immediate family. The next floor was a warren of guest rooms and suites, including an expansive suite housing the Lunts. "We did our best to install plumbing, so most of the bedrooms are *en suite*."

Lynn and Alfred murmured their delight.

They went back into the Old Manor from the terrace, and emerged in the front foyer behind the grand staircase. Alain took up the thread of his narrative with his back to the imposing front doors.

"To the left of the door here is a parlor which opens into the library. Originally, part of it was a dining area, but, over the centuries, many changes were made on that end of the house. Behind the library, the 'new' north wing was built at a right angle to the Old Manor to match the 'old' south wing of bedrooms built in the 1500s. The 'new' wing was built two hundred years after that."

They went through the parlor and the library beyond, and turned into the ground floor dining room. This was the first of the north wing's rooms. Behind the dining room stood the kitchens and pantries, moved up from the basement decades before, and updated with more modern equipment. The two floors above housed the staff, men on one floor and women on the other, though the staff was greatly diminished by this time, Alain lamented. First the Great War, and then this war depleted the supply of help even further. Though it was clear he was unhappy with the situation, he refrained from more than a sentence or two about that. "Who am I to begrudge those who wish to fight and die for this country?" Then he caught himself, his caustic tone fading away. "I do fervently hope we don't lose too many of our boys overseas."

Now, in the morning sun, Alain led them out of the dining room, emerging outside through the set of French doors on the north side of the room. They strolled along the side of the house, following a narrow paved walkway bordered by boxwood. They emerged beyond the end of the house on a sweep of grass that led down to the sea, which could be heard but not seen between an embracing cluster of trees swaying at the end of the lawn. He turned to face the house and swept his arm out to encompass the manor, glowing butter gold in the morning sun. "You can see the entire house from here. The Elizabethans put in the tall windows, which gives us a breathtaking view from the rooms that look out on this space."

Though she saw the terrace the day before, when they came out from the conservatory, Lynn wanted to effect a delayed reaction. It would strengthen her persona. "It's spectacular from this side as well!" The flagstone terrace sprawling from north wing to south wing meant a person could enter or leave the house from many points, and not get shoes or dress hems wet from dew. Or not get caught. "That terrace is big enough for dancing."

"Yes, we used to dance out here. It's actually best in the morning, with the sun coming up out there." Alain gestured to the far end of the lawn. "But there's room enough for both dancing and for the gardener to work his sorcery along the front end of the terrace and in the flower beds you see here." He turned toward the sound of the sea. "Let me show you a bit of the grounds."

The trio started off down the wide lawn, Alain commenting on the landscaping along either side of the lush green grass. He pointed to the left. "The garages and stables. We keep four horses, all suitable for riding. We never replaced the number of horses they stole for the Great War."

Lynn noticed the *stole*. More bitterness, more reason to ally himself with the Germans. She tucked her arm into Alain's elbow and matched his stride. "At least, they can't do that to you in this war. They've got iron horses now."

Alain nodded. "Tanks, yes." He fell silent for a moment, before regaining a bright face and gesturing to the right. "Over there, tucked into the trees, is our greenhouse. The gardener works there all through the seasons so we have a bountiful supply of flowers to bed in the summer."

Lynn withdrew her arm and clapped her hands. "Oh, Alain! We'd love to see the greenhouse. Alfred has *two* green thumbs, you know. We have a little farm–"

Alfred cut her off. "All in good time, Lynnie. I'm sure Alain isn't terribly interested in my meager attempts to till the soil." She knew his interruption was to more firmly cement her rambling conversation style.

"On the contrary, my good man," Alain said. "We are here to make your stay pleasant. If you wish to see our dirt..." He tilted his head and held out his arms. "Well, that can be arranged. But first, the view."

They continued walking toward the sea, which they could hear, but it was still out of sight.

"Do you have a nice beach?" Lynn asked.

Alain chuckled. "Willie took a stretch of coast to invade that included both cliff and beach, but over the years, land was snatched from my ancestors, and, of course, they took the choice beachfronts. We were left with the cliffs."

"Like Dover," Lynn said. "How impressive those cliffs are! Are yours too?"

"Judge for yourself," Alain said. They emerged on the clifftop with the Channel opening out in front of them.

Lynn gasped, a spontaneous honest gasp, at the waves rolling relentlessly toward them far below. She stayed away from the dropoff at the edge. "My! No chance of invasion here, I'd say." She watched Alain carefully to see how he'd react to that. She sighed. Perhaps it would give the impression of "too bad."

"No, I'd say not. No invasion here. Even Willie the Norman chose a different landfall," Alain said. "Much easier down the coast where there are better beachheads."

"Sounds like you've studied your history," Alfred said. "I wonder if the Germans ever thought of coming across?"

Lynn was suddenly very nervous at Alfred's foray into that fraught territory, but Alain simply turned away as if he didn't hear.

From the look on his face, though, Lynn surmised that he chose, rather, to play his cards close to the vest and refrain from commenting. She found that more telling than if he blustered about German invasions.

"You wanted to see the greenhouse?" Alain asked. "Let's do that tomorrow." He shaded his eyes and turned his face to the sky. "It appears clouds are moving in. This time of year, that often means rain, or at least drizzle." He lowered his hand. "Also, we're getting close to lunch, and Cook prefers we adhere to her midday schedule." He turned to Lynn. "Perhaps we can ride a bit this afternoon, if you'd like?" He opened his mouth to say something to Alfred, but Alfred beat him to it.

"Oh, no. Not me." Alfred held his hands out, seeming to push the idea away. "Lynn's the rider, not me. I'm quite content to stay behind with a script and a drink."

And the chance to poke around unencumbered, Lynn thought. *I know that ploy.* She grinned at Alain. "Then it will be the two of us tearing up the turf."

Alain's chuckle and nod sealed the deal.

-19-

Alain directed the ladies' maid to lay out jodhpurs and a tweed riding jacket for Lynn, along with smart leather gloves. When Lynn appeared at the stable, suitably clad, Alain bowed and handed her a helmet, velvety black with a cute button on the top to finish it off with whimsy. Lynn had a horse back at Ten Chimneys in Wisconsin, but did not have much of a chance to ride here in England. She was delighted with the familiar English saddle, and sure that the afternoon would be wildly successful, one way or another, even if Alfred couldn't scout the house properly.

Though Alain didn't own a huge rambling estate, the neighboring fields were open to riders, and the two of them took advantage to go far afield along the coastal cliff until it retreated and descended, leaving a skirt of beach stretched along the base, allowing just enough room for a small village to huddle in a tight cove.

The gallop out shifted to a gentle canter on the way back, but the wind and the necessity of watchful riding left few opportunities for conversation. They exchanged pleasure at the outing, handed the horses off to the stableboy, and headed into the house to change before meeting the other guests.

Lynn really hoped to garner more information on the ride with Alain, but she was frustrated in that venture. Ah, well. Nothing to be gained from that. Alfred didn't learn much of consequence either, other than discovering that apparently no part of the house, other than Alain's study, was restricted, though the help voiced concern over Alfred's ramblings in their territories. But Alfred, being his usual affable self, managed to captivate them with his interest and attention. However, no amount of charm could get him entrance into the secluded study. That left the pair with a determination to somehow enter that inner sanctum. It was no surprise that the lord's study was off limits. Almost everyone had a place just their own at home, where random visitors were barred. For Alfred, it was his chicken coop back at Ten Chimneys. He spent plenty of time exploring and researching how to raise chickens, so that he became the resident expert, an area Lynn surveyed from a distance. And happily, too.

After debriefing while they cleaned up and dressed, Lynn and Alfred left to rendezvous with the other guests and their host on the terrace. The clouds having dissipated, rain held off. Somehow, they would come up with a plan to get into the study. But for now, they needed to make an appearance with the others.

Afternoon tea was ready to be served, the terrace flagstones exuding warmth from being kissed by the sun off and on much of the day. Lynn could see several chaise longues inviting anyone to stretch out and bask while they waited for the help to deliver teacups and plates of petit fours and tiny sandwiches from the laden tea table.

The others were already there when Lynn and Alfred stepped out the French doors. The four gentlemen–business acquaintances, Alain assured them–fell into an immediate silence as the Lunts moved toward them. The two other couples, loading plates with sandwiches and biscuits, were close to the tea table and out of earshot of the others.

Alain stepped away from his quartet of men and called, "Here are the Celestials! Now our group is complete."

Lynn whispered to Alfred, "Notice how quiet they got when we appeared?"

Alfred leaned down, an intimate gesture really designed so he could reply. "We are famous, you know, darling."

She tilted her head back and looked at him with stars in her eyes. "Yes, darling, I do know that. But–" Alain was too close now for further conversation.

As if reading her mind, Lord Bufort said, "See how they fall under your spell? You appear like royals and everyone bows."

The looks they sent us feel more like resentment at having their discussion cut short. I wonder what exactly they were taking about? "Oh, I'm so sorry we stifled your business conversation," Lynn said. She brushed Alain's arm with her fingertips. "Please, don't let us interrupt."

"No, no, no," Alain protested, leading them to his companions. He turned to wave the two couples closer, though they were already hustling over to be introduced. "We are an intimate group, and all of us are so very excited about the reading you'll do for us tomorrow evening."

Introductions were made all around, and nothing seemed suspicious or askew. But then, it wouldn't, would it? Lynn quickly surmised that the two couples, introduced as friends from the area, were of little interest to their espionage quest. She read them as star-struck, here mainly to meet the famous couple. Nothing belied Lynn's sense on that regard. Besides, they would not be spending the night, but were close enough to go home and return the following evening, chauffeured by Lord Bufort's driver, the man supplied with enough gas rationing cards to be generous.

Lynn listened carefully to the ebb and flow of conversation, none of which rose beyond the level of gardening, the difficulties of getting help, the always-looming problems of rationing. Here, in this tiny corner, the bombings so prevalent in other parts of England, particularly the major cities and industrial areas, seemed a minor threat. Not forgotten, surely, but only indirectly molding life here at Forest Hall.

Lynn made it a point to talk to each guest individually. Perhaps that might yield a tidbit of useful information. The two couples gave her nothing. They were more interested in piling on adulation about the Lunts' theatrical lives. She listened politely, gushed thanks, spoke briefly about backstage doings, but gave them nothing but fluff. No talk of Pip's death or the horrible aftermaths of the continuing bombings. No talk of their work as spotters and wardens and hospital volunteers. It was made quite clear that this was to be a hiatus from rubble and air raid sirens and bodies huddled in shelters, or worse, dying in the streets.

Lynn moved on.

The Quartet, as she thought of them, stuck rather close to Alain, so little chance to charm any of them. That in itself raised Lynn's suspicions. If she and Alfred were to ferret out Alain's plans or movements on behalf of the Nazis, wouldn't it be feasible that he would invite like-minded sympathizers to his country house, and keep them close? It was clear that he couldn't be inviting German invasion from across the Channel. His cliff would preclude that happening on his property. But that didn't mean he wasn't part of some other conspiracy. Time would tell. And time was running out. It was Tuesday already, and they were slated to leave Forest Hall Thursday, to get back to London for an afternoon rehearsal before their Friday performance. Could they truly find out in such a short time the threads Lord Bufort was sending out?

A breakthrough presented itself when Alfred wandered off to apparently pursue his own line of questioning with one of the couples. The quietest of the Quartet took himself off to one side to light his cigarette where the breeze was of no consequence. The others were deep in conversation about the possibility of getting a side of pig that was slated to be slaughtered at a nearby farm.

"I love this time of day, don't you?" Lynn moved like a border collie cutting out a single sheep for the shepherd. She positioned herself between the man with his cigarette case and his companions. Her talk would be loud enough for them to hear, assuring them that no danger came from her.

He nodded, busy with lighting his cigarette. Once that task was successful, he held out his gunmetal silver cigarette case to her.

She shook her head. "I tried them once, but they do terrible things to my voice. So, I swore off." She held up her hand, palm out.

He smiled and clicked the case shut, sliding it into his pocket. But not before Lynn caught a glimpse of something raised on the cover. An eagle with outspread wings, grasping...something. She couldn't see more, couldn't see a wreath or a swastika. But she recognized Hitler's German eagle. How foolish of the man to bring such a case into the country, much less use it! But her gaze swept away to look toward the sea, and her face remained placid, without reaction.

She turned back. "I'm sorry. I didn't catch your name." She extended a hand. "Lynn Fontanne."

He grasped it with a firm handshake. "Oh, I know you, Miss Fontanne–"

"Lynn, please. Herr?" Would that get a rise? She hoped he would buy her ditzy demeanor.

It did, and he did. But it was so subtle, anyone but Lynn would miss it. His hand in hers retreated a miniscule amount, and his face froze halfway to an open smile. Instead, it turned into a penetrating look, not a glare, but leaning toward wary.

"Mister. Mister Block." His face softened and he gave her hand a final squeeze before letting go. "But please call me René."

"Do I detect a French accent, René?" Lynn tilted her head and sent him a coy smile out from under her eyelids.

"Paris, yes. I'm from Paris. A most beautiful city."

No, you're not, Lynn countered. *You're not from Paris. I hear Alsace, not Paris.* Alsace-Lorraine, the territories tossed back and forth like a shuttlecock between France and Germany, were once more in

German hands, as of 1940, though still titularly French. Here was a man with an Alsatian accent, and, considering the evidence of the cigarette case, a German sympathizer. A Nazi sympathizer.

Lynn recovered in a blink. "I love Paris as well. Before the war, Alfred and I came over every summer to procure couturier dresses and such for our next season productions. That and, of course, to bask in the City of Light. Wandering the boulevards, finding little cafes to sit and sip tea or a cognac, people-watching, generally." She was so tempted to slip in something false about Paris to see his reaction, but that would be a fool's errand. It would certainly raise suspicion on his part. Besides, she had enough evidence with his German-French accent, to say nothing of the cigarette case, to seal her convictions. She tucked it all away to share with Alfred later. She could see her companion growing a bit impatient. He no longer tilted his head toward her, and his gaze flitted like a bird from her to something, or someone, behind her on the terrace.

Deciding to put him out of his misery, she gave a bell-like laugh. "I've cornered you long enough." The word choice was deliberate. "I fear I've deserted my husband as well. So delightful to chat with you, René." She touched him on the sleeve.

René offered the usual platitudes about how pleased he was, then gave a truncated bow and darted away.

Lynn was quite pleased with herself. A fine role, played to perfection. Not too high, not too low. And she came away with an unexpected bit of information. She accepted a glass of champagne from a steward making the rounds with his silver tray, giving him a smile and a gracious nod as she traded her teacup for the wine.

Making her way across the terrace, she sharpened her hearing as she neared the Quartet, now clustered together again. Before they fell silent as she passed, she caught a cluster of words said *sotto voce*, not the usual volume for an innocent afternoon tea hour.

"...night...maps...ready...meet?...outside..."

The words held little sense at the moment, but Lynn could feel in her bones that they must be fraught with meaning. Like mere ink marks on the page of a script, once delivered, they could take on a power and depth. Given enough time to consult with Alfred, she hoped they could bring the words to life.

Within a dozen or so steps, Alfred appeared at her elbow. He bent to kiss her cheek, whispering as his lips passed her ear. "Learn anything?"

Again, she gave out a laugh like a crystal bell. "Of course, darling. René Block–" She gave a soft German ending to his last name. "–delights in Paris, just as we do." Her voice dropped to a mere breath. "We must get into the study. Tonight."

"Anything you want, my dear," Alfred said, the volume natural, but certainly loud enough for anyone near to hear. "I serve to please."

-20-

The evening was long after dinner, and Lynn was getting impatient with small talk. She knew no one could see any of that in her demeanor, but this role wore on her more than with any stage performance. Of course, more depended on this stage than on any of the others.

Tonight was a chance to try and get into Alain's study. From what Lynn heard, the Quartet and Alain would be busy meeting...somewhere. Somewhere outside of the Old Manor, from the sound of what she heard earlier. That gave them an opportunity, one that must not be passed up. They had a reading to give tomorrow evening, so that ruled out exploring the study then. Everyone might be wide awake and talkative until the wee hours. And daylight was impossible. Too much movement of staff, guests, and, worst of all, Lord Buford, during the day. One could hardly turn around without encountering someone, or hearing unfamiliar noises that set Lynn's teeth on edge. She saw Alfred heading her way.

Alfred sidled up. "Looking a bit pale, my dear. Are you feeling quite all right?" He set down his cognac snifter before turning to put his arm along her waist.

Lynn dropped her shoulders and weakened her knees in an immediate response to what she intuited as the prelude to an invasion of the study. "I am a bit tired, Alfred." They both modulated their voices enough so those nearby would hear. "Maybe I have a touch of...something." She didn't want to commit to anything specific.

"Take your time, my dear," Alfred whispered into her ear.

She heeded his advice by wilting gradually, not suddenly, so as to make their retreat believable. She relaxed her shoulders, exhaled with chin tilted up a bit and mouth open, tried out a wan smile. Then, a little rally, straightening her spine, setting her glass on a nearby table, and patting her hair. She faded into a nearby chair.

Anyone approaching saw a woman declining step by miniscule step into fatigue, and perhaps even nausea. She let her arms droop loose on the arms of the chair, as if she were running out of energy to lift them even for a sip at the drink sitting next to her.

After a few rounds of the room, chatting with other guests while sending an obvious glance her way, Alfred returned to stay by her side, bending low to murmur a "how are you feeling" every once in a while. Finally, he said, with quite a bit more volume, "Perhaps we should make our apologies and retire for the evening."

Good. He read her cues in perfect harmony. "Oh, darling, I think you're probably right. A good night's sleep should do wonders." Lynn stood and laid her head on Alfred's shoulder.

For his part, he put his arm around her. "Come, let's explain to Alain and get you to bed."

Lynn knew she couldn't make her face pale on command, but as they made their way to take their leave of their host, Lynn let her face muscles relax and sag a bit. She dropped her chin just a tiny bit to imply a feeling of fatigue, or the onset of some as yet undefined illness.

"Of course, you must take care of yourself, Lynn," Alain assured her as they explained their departure at an earlier hour than usual. "Should I send up some tea? Or perhaps something else?"

Lynn shook her head, careful to move with lethargy.

Alain sent them off, Alfred's arm supporting his wife.

The moment the door closed behind them, Lynn recovered, and headed across the foyer and down the corridor toward Alain's study. She whispered, "Good thing the stairway is close, just in case someone comes along. We can explain we got lost."

Alfred hurried along beside her. "Not good, Lynnie. Better to say you were headed for that little toilet next to his study. More believable."

They reached the study door without incident. Lynn held her breath, crossed her fingers, and set her hand on the doorknob. The knob was frozen in place, locked. In despair, Lynn set her forehead on the door. The door inched forward.

"Locked," Lynn hissed, "but not latched!" A miracle, without a doubt. Alfred wouldn't have to apply his dubious lockpicking skills. She herself was no better, even under Hamilton's tutelage. She heard Alfred give out a great exhale.

They slipped in and closed the door behind them, sliding it into its frame without even a click of the latch. They could leave the door as they found it, and slip away quickly as well.

"I'll take the desk," Alfred said. "You search whatever else you can."

"Did you bring the little camera?" She knew it was a foolish question. Alfred never forgot anything. His attention to detail was phenomenal, and tonight was no exception, a fact cemented with the curt nod of his head.

Lynn left him lifting papers and opening drawers as she rounded the room, looking with hands and eyes for anything pointing to the lord's activities. She found nothing. But within a very few minutes, she heard a soft "Aha!" from Alfred's direction. After noting where she stopped rummaging, she rushed to join him at the desk. He was already snapping a picture.

He whispered, "Not sure what this shows, but it was tucked away in a drawer, under other papers that looked pretty innocuous. We'll let James determine what's what."

"A map, Alfred." Lynn pointed to a sheet Alfred was flattening, ready to photograph. "That's a portion of the English coast. And it's a part that's not very far from here, I think. What on earth?"

Alfred frowned, leaned close, and snapped the shutter on the little camera.

"Look at all those marks." As Alfred stood up, she peered closer. "Those are lines." Her index finger hovered over the map, following the fine tracings. "Connecting... Oh, Alfred, they're connecting points in France to points along the coast, the southeast coast, across from Calais!"

Alfred joined her close examination. "Look here, Lynnie. Down along the edge. It looks like the paper was cut or torn along that side. Isn't that–"

"Two bent legs of a swastika."

"That's what I'm seeing too." Alfred aimed the camera at the paper's edge, moved in closer and snapped another photo.

"A German invasion? Surely, they wouldn't be so foolish." Lynn's voice didn't sound very confident.

"The Germans planned it three years ago, but it didn't fly at the time. This makes it look like they're going to try again. The paper's too fresh to be an old plan."

"Or–"

"Or it's an Allied plan as to where to land troops on the French coast."

Lynn looked horror-struck. "We can't just take them. Alain would surely miss the map."

"Hence, the camera." Alfred flourished the camera.

She blew out a breath, and reached to ease the map out of the way. "What about those other papers? The ones underneath."

A sound from the corridor made them both freeze.

Voices and laughter bubbled up, gaining in volume as someone–several someones, from the sound of it–drew closer.

Alfred dropped the camera into his pocket with one hand and gathered the map and loose papers with the other. With barely time to straighten the jumble, he jammed everything in the drawer where he found them, and closed it.

Lynn, frantic, spared only a moment to look at Alfred. He would have to devise his own way.

She ran for the sofa on the other side of the room and threw herself down. She had just enough time to arrange herself, one foot still set on the floor. One arm up over her forehead. The other arm draped down to the floor. She felt her fingers brush the edge of a piece of paper under the sofa as her hand dropped. No time. Eyes closed. A drop of the chin. She knew Alfred would adapt to any situation she could present.

Alfred was breathing heavily as he crashed to his knees beside her. She slid her eyes open just enough to see him hovering over her. A most welcome sight. "Under," she mouthed, knowing Alfred blocked Alain's view. "Grab." She hoped with all her heart Alfred understood her signals. This was really no time to test their union, but it couldn't be helped.

She felt his shoulder drop, the shoulder farthest from the study door. Which, from the sound, was being opened.

Alfred touched her hand. Not a moment to spare for words. No way to tell if he got her message.

Lord Bufort's voice boomed in. "I want you to see–" Sudden silence.

"Alain." Alfred's voice. He grasped Lynn's hand and twisted his body toward the door. She could feel it. Hopefully, there was enough movement there to mask him hiding the...whatever it was...somewhere on him. "So sorry to have invaded your inner sanctum. Lynn almost fainted in the hall, and this door was the closest. Luckily, the door wasn't locked. Well, it was locked, but it wasn't latched. I pushed and it just popped open. I thought I'd better bring her in until she felt clearer in the head. Then we could get upstairs without her tumbling down the steps in a sudden faint."

Lynn recognized his rambling as a deliberate effort to deflect attention. It was time to rescue him. She drew her arm away from her forehead with a languid movement and opened her eyes to half-mast. "I think I'm feeling better, Alfred. Would you help me sit up, please?" She noticed that Alain stood stock still just inside the doorway, with at least two of the Quartet peering around him at the Lunt's tableau.

She hoped Alain was sufficiently fooled. He stepped closer to them and made solicitous noises. "Oh, my dear! What a turn for the worse!" His face didn't betray too much worry over their presence, though Lynn detected the remnants of a frown between his eyebrows.

You have no idea, Lynn thought. But she sent out a feeble smile as Alfred put his arm around her, and offered a hand as well to help her sit up. Once upright, she rested her head on the back of the sofa, not wanting to appear completely normal again without a buildup. She sighed. "I am so very sorry, Alain." She sent him a soft glance, chin lifted, eyes a bit hooded, the bare hint of a smile on her lips. The look which charmed everyone she met, from princes to paupers.

"I just hope you're all right," the lord said, bending towards her.

Alfred was all Knight in Shining Armor, not letting anyone, much less the dragon himself, get close enough to scorch. "I'm sure she'll be fine." He turned to his wife. "Do you think you're recovered enough to go up the stairs?"

She nodded, looking up into his eyes, those dear eyes. "I believe so, darling." *Not a moment too soon.* "We mustn't keep Alain out of his own study any longer." She patted her hair, took a deep breath, mouth open, and accepted Alfred's gesture to help her stand up.

Alfred tucked her hand into the crook of his elbow. "Take your time, Lynnie. We wouldn't want you keeling over again."

"Yes, take all the time you need," Alain said. "Don't rush. You're welcome to sit a while longer, just to be sure."

Lynn heard his voice giving him away. He was anxious to get them out of the study. *Don't worry. I'm just as delighted to leave as you are to remove us from these premises.* But she didn't say that, of course.

Instead, she cooed, "You are far too kind, Alain. We'll just go on up to bed."

Alfred led her off. Just for effect, she kept one hand busy tucking loose strands of hair back in place.

They didn't drop their roles of invalid and helpful companion until they were safely back in their suite.

Before they did anything else, they swept around the room, criss-crossing in front of and behind each other in search of any evidence that someone could listen in through, say, a peephole in the wallpaper. With both of them looking, they could go over every nook and cranny twice.

Their hunt complete, they faced each other and shrugged, arms out and palms out in that recognizable gesture. Lynn didn't even want to risk saying, "Nothing." Alfred nodded.

They undressed in silence, though they were reasonably sure the room was secure. In spite of that, Lynn found her fingers fumbling with buttons, and her muscles were so tense she was trembling.

Once Alfred joined her in bed and pulled her close to him, Lynn stopped shaking. She curled tight to his side, feeling his arm sheltering her and his warmth reassuring her she was safe. By unspoken agreement, they only whispered.

Lynn put her lips to Alfred's ear. "Did you get it?" If her message was received, he knew what she meant.

He nodded. "I managed to cram it into my cummerbund." He reached into his pajama top's pocket and edged the tip of... What would he pull out? "Envelope," he whispered. He moved to pull it out completely, but Lynn set a hand on his pocket.

"No. Save it. Someone will be looking for it, I'm afraid. We have to get it out of here."

Alfred patted his pocket. "Right now, it's safe." His voice was barely discernable. He settled the envelope deeper.

"I hope it's worth something. It seemed to be forgotten. Or maybe Alain felt that was a safer spot, under the sofa. Either way, you found plenty of other information."

"I really wanted to get more photos," Alfred said. "I couldn't tell what was on the other papers, but I'm sure it was not letters to Mama." Even in the apparent safety of their room, and using only whispers, his tone was rough with consternation.

Lynn patted his chest. "Don't worry, darling. I'm sure that map is going to be enough for..." She thought better of saying names out loud. "Maybe we can try again tomorrow night." She felt Alfred shaking his head.

"I'm sure we'll never get in that study again, Lynnie. Even if he doesn't suspect us of nefarious dealings, he's sure to make sure that the study, and probably the desk too, is locked tight as a drum. If that map says what we think it does, it's far too dangerous to leave the room unlocked."

She sighed. "You're probably right. I just hope what we've got is enough."

"I know what you mean. But we still have tomorrow. Maybe we'll find out more, if we keep our eyes open."

Lynn smiled in spite of herself. "We always keep our eyes open, Alfred." She shifted even closer to him. "Maybe we can find something on the grounds. Alain promised us a tour of the greenhouse tomorrow. Who knows what we can turn up?" She showed him her fingers crossed in the well-worn sign of hope.

"Not turnips, I hope." Alfred yawned.

Lynn snickered. "Agreed. But enough of the jokes, darling. I need my beauty sleep if we're exploring again tomorrow. No time to do more tonight."

There was little response from Alfred. Only deep breathing, and the hint of a snore.

-21-

Wednesday dawned bright and clear, with no wind at all. The soft susurration of the sea could be heard drifting up from far away down the lawn. From the dining room, the guests were directed to the courtyard terrace, protected, like a mother's arms, by the wings of the manor house. Breakfast would be alfresco in the warm sunlight of a spring morning free of the usual breezes and the notorious English weather. That didn't preclude the need for jackets and scarves, as everyone quickly discovered. Lynn and Alfred met the Quartet, gabbing away, coming in to collect warmer clothes.

"You should better go back for a jacket and a hat," René, the purported Parisian, said, as they approached the Lunts in the lower hallway. "It might be here April, but it is not like Spain." He chuckled at his own attempt at a joke.

Lynn recognized the rhythm of a non-native speaker, and certainly not the fluted rhythms of a resident of Paris. Alsace, again. She was more than convinced that he was really of German descent. She was an astute listener, and well able to respond without hesitation without giving herself away. "I shall do just that," she said, giving him a little salute. She pivoted to follow the Quartet. "Come on, Alfred. We should heed their advice. It's obviously cooler out than we anticipated. We'll look ever so forward-thinking if we appear in our coats and mufflers." She was well aware that the mysterious envelope was secure in the money belt around Alfred's waist, hidden where no one could see it, or even guess it was there. They agreed he would never take it off until they were back in London.

"Right behind you, my dear," Alfred said, following behind like an obedient valet.

In their room, Lynn swept up her double-breasted lightweight grey wool coat and cinched the belt, rather than buttoning up the front. Alfred grabbed his favorite long camel jacket. He was about to step out the door when Lynn wiggled her finger at his head. "Take a hat, darling."

He backtracked and picked up his taupe hat sitting on a side table. "Doesn't match, but it'll keep the wind off."

Lynn loved the hat, even the pinch in the front, making it look like the prow of a ship. She always melted when he put it on, tilted it over one eye, and winked. She really loved him more than she loved the hat, of course. But it certainly enhanced his desireability. "I hope I can keep my hands off of you," she said.

"I hope you can't." Alfred winked and slipped out the door.

With that, they headed for the staircase.

Suitably accoutered, they returned to the lower hallway and exited to the courtyard, where the servants set up a table with chafing dishes of eggs, rashers, potatoes, black pudding, and fried tomatoes. Lynn remembered Alain mentioning chickens somewhere on the estate, allowing them more than the usual supply of eggs, the same as the Savoy Hotel back in London, which had their own chicken coops. Luxury, by any standard.

Lynn was distracted from her thoughts of circumventing ration cards by one of the serving women, hands gloved, coming around with a teapot covered in a knitted cozy.

Lynn made a beeline for the tea. Cup secured, and hands wrapped around the cup, Lynn stepped to greet Alain. "What a

grand idea, Alain, to serve breakfast outdoors. Such a lovely day!"
She lifted her cup to take a sip, never taking her eyes from her host.

"I simply couldn't resist the sunshine." Alain's enthusiasm was
belied by his hands, which were stuffed deeply in his pockets. "We
get so few of these days here on the coast, so we must take
advantage where we can."

"Alain, come join us!" Alfred called for the lord and Lynn to join
him at a nearby table. The Quartet were at the buffet table, filling
their plates amid a flurry of ongoing conversation, apparently
lighthearted, based on their smiles and relaxed demeanors.

Lynn breathed a silent thanks. Hopefully, Alain was not
suspicious at all over their antics in his study the evening before.
Had the Germans been briefed? The Quartet was not looking
askance at the Lunts, or even peering over their shoulders, only
pealing out loud laughter at some private joke. They weren't
attempting to direct attention to something inane, such as the
clouds or the birds. It seemed that all was well.

Lynn realized she had decelerated to a turtle's pace, causing
Alain to almost collide with her. She picked up her pace and turned
to him with an abashed look. "Oh, excuse me! I was so taken with
the daffodils along the woods, I simply didn't pay attention to what
I was doing."

"Quite all right, Lynn." Alain removed his hands from coat
pockets and waved a greeting to Alfred. "Enjoy the buffet. My
chickens will be delighted if you appreciate their contributions." He
didn't seem upset.

Lynn set a hand on his sleeve. "Speaking of other guests, where
are the lovely couples we met? I assume they trained in
from...somewhere?" She was fishing.

Alain chuckled. "No, those were neighbors, or at least, folks I
know quite well from the village. They went back home last night.
So, here we are, just us." Alain's sweep of a gesture took in anyone
in the courtyard.

"I've met René," Lynn said, "but I didn't catch the names of the other three." *Because they were never offered,* she added to herself.

"Ah! So sorry." Alain gave a smart little bow. "René's friend–from Switzerland, by the way–is Bruno. The other two are Alec and David, British to the bone. But we all share the same dedication to ending this war."

I'm sure, Lynn thought. *Just not with the Allies winning.* But her smile retained its softness and her eyes their wide-eyed interest. She lowered her chin, but maintained eye contact. Let Alain read into it what he would. "We all are desperate for the end of war." She looked across at the four guests at the buffet. Yes, they were the only ones remaining here at Forest Hall.

Alfred and her. And the Quartet. Beguiled Brits and two Germans, say what you will about France and Switzerland. She reminded herself to stop thinking of them that way. Too easy to slip up. As far as anyone knew, they were simply a clutch of friends from the Continent. Two of them looked too military to be simple friends who escaped the claws of the Nazis. The other two looked bland enough, here in the morning sunlight. No high-stepping gait, no leather trench coats, no fedoras hiding their faces.

Lynn sighed. Could she and Alfred even find out anything more about these...questionable men, before they themselves returned to London? They had only this one day. Their train left early the next morning.

She crossed the flagstones to join Alfred, who rose to meet her.

"Let's go pile on some breakfast, shall we?" he said. "I'm starving."

Lynn set her cup on the table and took Alfred's arm. "Me too. You know how I love breakfast." She gave him a wink.

They polished off their platefuls of hot food, and were adding strawberry jam to their toast, when Alain strode over and joined them. He gestured for the maid to top off their tea. "Lynn looks refreshed," he said to Alfred. "Better than she did last night." He leaned down and grasped her hand. "Do you think you'll be feeling well enough to do our planned play reading tonight? Last night you really scared me."

Lynn tensed, concerned that Alain's words covered more than simple comments. What exactly scared him last night? That they found something incriminating in his study? That she and Alfred were a danger to him? Or to his plans? Was that fear enough to turn him against them? Hopefully, he was only expressing concern over her sudden illness. Her mind raced.

He found them in his private study, after all, Lynn incapacitated on the sofa. At least, that's what he was supposed to see. Was her performance believable? Never had a scene been so crucial, nor needed to be executed so flawlessly. Now, this morning, she did her best to keep her face relaxed, her eyes rather hooded, her free hand curled in her lap. Did he realize...? She needed a diversion. Luckily, Alfred was already providing just that.

Alain released Lynn's hand and stood up straight.

"I hope we didn't throw a monkey wrench into your plans," Alfred said. "Luckily, she just needed a good night's sleep. She's been working very, very hard. You know she's an air raid warden in London. Put that on top of our madcap schedule on stage, and you can see why she just collapsed from exhaustion. Everything caught up to her. We are so grateful you could offer us some time away here to recuperate."

Lynn appreciated his technique of running off at the mouth. She raised her cup in a salute, to slow Alfred's rush of words. "Very grateful, Alain. And I'm back on top of my form. All rested and ready for today." She sent Alain a sideways glance and smile that came close to flirting. "And didn't you promise to show us your greenhouse? I know Alfred would be so thrilled. He's the gardener in the family, you know. I'm surprised he hasn't been out digging around in your flower beds already."

She cringed inwardly. She sincerely hoped Alain wouldn't be put on guard about Alfred digging into anything around the estate.

Which is exactly what they were doing, of course. Time to smile and put on a vacuous look.

Alain chuckled. "I'd be delighted to show you around the greenhouse. I'm very proud of it, you know. Our head gardener should be around after lunch, in case you would like to pick his brain."

"Sounds delightful," Lynn said. She turned to Alfred. "Doesn't it sound delightful, darling? You could get some ideas for flowers too. I know you like English vegetable seeds better than American seeds, so maybe flower seeds are better too."

"I'd sure appreciate seeing what you're growing, Alain," Alfred said.

"Then it's settled. We'll head down to the greenhouse after lunch. We'll have time then. We can make the rounds of the grounds on the way too. I know you've seen some of what we have, but maybe now you'd like to take a closer look, seeing as how you're really into getting your hands dirty."

Alfred laughed. "You found one of my favorite things to do. Get up early and weed. Back at Ten Chimneys, they all think I'm crazy. Well, some do. Lynn is not an early riser, but she is a prime example of why they call it beauty sleep."

Lynn cooed some incoherent nothings and lowered her chin. She looked up from under hooded eyes at her beloved husband. "You say the sweetest things, Alfred."

Alain stood up. "I'll leave you two to your romancing. If it suits you, we'll meet right here in the courtyard after luncheon. Say two o'clock? I think we'll dine indoors. We face east here, but the sun may not be direct enough later to warm us." With a wave of his hand, he turned away and went to join the Quartet, who were enjoying tea and coffee amid the detritus of their heavy breakfasts.

Lynn and Alfred headed indoors, choosing to enter via the conservatory door, which meant they had to walk down the hallway past the "new" toilet and Alain's study before emerging in the grand foyer, where they could trek up the staircase to their suite.

This was not without thought, however. They were determined, even without voicing it to each other, to try for access to the study.

As they passed through the conservatory, Lynn took special note of the lush Boston fern on its stand near a statue of a girl poised with a tipped urn of water that burbled as it dripped into a marble basin below. Something to comment on, should they be questioned as to why they were in that particular hallway.

Lynn dawdled near the indoor steps up into the main house, as Alfred strode down the corridor toward the study door. If anyone came in, she would be able to alert her husband. She knew, without asking, that he would most likely use the excuse of finding the toilet, while she waited in that lovely spot, admiring the greenery and flowers.

As sure as if they wrote the scene themselves, two of the Quartet, but not the faux Parisian, came toward them on the terrace. As soon as one noticed Lynn fingering a feathery palm leaf, he nudged his companion, and they walked toward the conservatory door.

Lynn, already on high alert, turned, sent them a surprised and delighted look, and went to the door to let them in. She squealed in delight. *There, that should be loud enough.* "So good to see you two taking the sun this lovely morning. Did you get enough to eat? Wasn't the buffet just the best? I wonder where the lord manages to get potatoes this time of year. Alfred's sometimes go bad over the winter."

"What are you telling them about my potatoes?" Alfred's voice cascaded down over her shoulder as he set his hand on her back.

The touch of his hand was the prop she needed to keep from sagging from the tension. "All set, Alfred?" She turned to him, but only far enough so she could keep the two men in her peripheral vision.

"A bit too much coffee, my dear. Just glad Alain's ancestors put a toilet close at hand."

How discreet he was. Not even the twitch of an eyebrow. Lynn noticed that he didn't look down at her, but watched the men instead. "Well, then. Let's upstairs. I could use a little time to look over our script for this coming weekend's show." She gave him a gentle tap on the chest. "We've been derelict in our duties, Alfred." This time she looked fully at the two other men. "We simply must keep rehearsing, you know. Sometimes he comes up with the most brilliant ideas to make a scene more believable." Best to stop talking. She didn't want the Quartet to start thinking of the Lunts as always "onstage," though that's often what they were when dealing with the public.

"Time to get to work," Alfred said. "She can be a slave driver." He took her elbow and steered her around to head down the hall to the foyer. Not another word was spoken between them.

Lynn heard the two men leave the conservatory and go back out to the terrace, their voices fading as they left. The glass-paned French door shivered a glissando as they closed it behind them. She exhaled a puff of air and relaxed her neck.

Alfred set a finger on his lips, then pulled her to a halt before the study door. He barely touched the doorknob, but it was enough to show Lynn that, just as they suspected, the door was now locked. Lynn shrugged and shook her head. Alfred nodded.

Upon reaching their room, the Lunts put their heads close together to discuss what they might be able to do in order to ferret out more information about Alain's connection with the Nazis. It didn't take long, as they both were at a dead end in that area. No access to the study, no way to lever information out of the Quartet. Things looked rather bleak on that front.

"Hamilton is going to regret asking for our help," Alfred said. "We don't have much to offer."

"At least we have your...things," Lynn said. "And–" She stopped herself.

Alfred patted the inner pocket in his jacket, where he carried the camouflaged camera. "I hope we'll have a chance to use it again. Time is running out to uncover anything else, though."

"I know, darling. Tomorrow, the train." She raised one eyebrow. "Maybe the greenhouse will yield something. Maybe it's a secret radio station, or a hidden armory." She pulled her head forward and her shoulders up, leaving an impression of a vulture on the hunt.

Alfred laughed. "You are the most interesting woman I know, Lynnie. You're always looking for another side to things." He tilted his head back and sighed. "Until we can go forward somehow, we should spend some time rehearsing. Always room for improvements."

They used the remainder of the morning hours to go over their roles for the forthcoming London weekend performances. In actuality, there was little to do, little to perfect. But their dedication to their craft often found them haggling, or at least rehashing, how they could make the moments better. No wonder people called them the Fabulous Lunts.

-22-

Lunch was hot pasties, in keeping with the drop in temperature as the winds shifted and the sound of heavier seas reached those who ventured outdoors. The Quartet finished eating, stood, made their apologies for retreating to the library to discuss some impending business, and exited the dining room without another word.

Lynn was left with a sour taste in her mouth, she was so sure they were planning something she wanted to know about. That would be impossible, of course. The Quartet didn't warm much to the Lunts, but kept to themselves, and would certainly not welcome any kind of intrusion.

"Are you sure you want to see the gardens and grounds?" Alain asked, breaking into her thoughts. "It's a bit more intemperate out there now. The grass is still wet from the rain shower last night."

"No forecast of rain for this afternoon," Alfred said, "so we should be all right, as long as we wear mackintoshes."

"And our Wellies," Lynn said.

"Boots are in the mud room next to the kitchen," Alain said. "We can pick them up on the way out that way. If you're still willing to traipse around in the weather?"

"Nothing out of the ordinary yet," Lynn said, "and Alfred has been known to plunge outside in rain so heavy the horses seek shelter, just to make sure his garden isn't drowning. We'll be fine."

"I checked, and it looks like the clouds will all lift away later in the afternoon, and tonight and tomorrow should be crystal clear..."

Alain's voice faded into ghosts, as Lynn's thoughts spiraled off. If the night skies were clear, as predicted, she felt a stab of sympathy for the Londoners sure to suffer another night of bombings. She mentally shook herself, and Alfred's voice came into focus.

"We'll be indoors in your greenhouse," Alfred was saying. "If this wicked war ever ends, I'd like to see about getting a small greenhouse for Ten Chimneys. Give me a headstart on bedding seedlings. Tomatoes, and–"

Lynn was back in control of her thoughts. She cut him off at the pass. "Don't get him started, Alain, or we'll never get out." She ran her fingers down Alfred's arm, and he reached out to take her hand and kiss it. No offense taken by Alfred. She knew he would not be upset at the interruption.

"Right. Just so," Alain said, pushing his chair back from the table. "Let's get changed into warmer clothes and meet in the mudroom beyond the kitchen. No one will mind if we go on through."

Alain was pulling on his Wellies when Lynn and Alfred appeared in the mudroom. Lynn, dressed in woolen trousers and a shooting jacket, pulled a cloche down tight over her hair, ensuring even her ears were protected.

"You look like you're ready for a fox hunt," Alain said, then turned to Alfred. "I'm delighted we had extra cool-weather clothing that fits."

"Well, the pants are a little short." Alfred looked down. "But the wool socks are great, and the boots will cover it all." He swung a jacket on, and accepted a stalker cap from Alain, which he crammed onto his head. "This'll do just fine." He turned up the collar of the jacket and maneuvered his shoulders to settle everything in place.

"Just untie the flaps on top, if your ears get cold," Alain said. "It's a fine woolen cap."

Lynn said, "I remember all those wool socks and such we sent to London for the troops before America got involved in the war." She stopped herself. No need for Alain to know how widely and desperately they supported the Allied efforts *pro bono*. Both of them working the Stage Door Canteen in New York, Lynn's recording of a poignant nationalistic poem, Alfred's cooking lessons, to say nothing of the myriad packages sent to relatives and friends in London, and the war bond sales they touted.

Although, when she thought about it, Alain probably already knew everything about them. She fervently hoped he was focused more on their theater contributions than anything else. After all, he considered himself a true theater aficionado. As far as she could tell when they were in London, theater really was the only thing on his mind when in the city. Now that they were in his country enclave, she saw that he divided his attention. The Lunts were important, yes, but the Quartet seemed every bit as significant as they were, if not more. Understandable, if he were trying to undermine the Allied war efforts by supporting the Nazis.

Alfred snapped her out of her reverie. "Are you coming, Lynnie? Or are you going to spend the afternoon lost in the clouds?"

"Coming!" she called. The others were already outside, but she heard Alfred tell Alain, "Sometimes I wonder if she hears what I say."

Lynn knew perfectly well that she was attuned to Alfred, and he himself was well aware of that. But again, this might be a trait she could use. If Alain thought she was a flibbertigibbet, he might discount her ability to hear things she shouldn't. One could only hope.

Enough ruminating. She stabbed her feet into Wellies and hurried out to join the men, who were already almost halfway across the lawn.

Lynn reached them in time to hear Alain mention the folly built just into the woods that ran along the right side of the lawn. Following his arm's aim, Lynn could just make out the columns and dome of the small structure, nestled among the trees, and almost obscured by the new spring greenery. The lines were too rigid to be tree trunks and the dome a clear marker of something built, rather than grown.

They moved with relief from the wind to admire the tidy folly.

"A generation or two ago, the owner decided to allow the wild ivy to creep up. That meant that the jungle tried to reclaim its birthright, and we almost lost the folly."

"It looks quite recovered now," Lynn said. "Do you use it for anything? Picnics and such?" Fishing again.

Alain shook his head. "Too exposed to the weather. There's only the dome above, as you can see. No walls, only columns. We found nothing here when we cleaned it all up, and we've left it that way. A simple folly to tease the eyes. Although, my wife used to sit on the steps here in the heat of summer to read a bit. She claimed the breezes were refreshing. But I found it simply too damp, being so close to the Channel." He led them back to the lawn.

They skirted the woods until they reached the wide, manicured grass path to the greenhouse. "Still rather windy here, isn't it?" Alfred said, as the greenhouse loomed in sight. "No problem with losing glass panels to the gusts?"

"No," Alain said. "The only detriment seems to be that you can't hear the dinner bell down here." He chuckled. "Of course, with rationing now, maybe that's not such a loss."

Lynn found that preposterous, considering the relative bounty of the lord's table, in spite of rationing. Money could find a way. But she smiled. A small one, but one designed to show she understood, and sympathized with, the privations here at Forest Hall.

Alfred gripped her elbow at that moment, throwing her thoughts out the window. He squeezed, a sure signal that she might be missing something. Ah, yes! A call to dinner from the Old Manor was too distant to be heard in the greenhouse, which meant sounds in the greenhouse couldn't be heard at the Old Manor either. Message received. A small–albeit, very small–gift to know that tidbit. They could no longer get into the study, and from the broken conversation Lynn heard earlier, there must be another, more discrete place to meet. Perhaps the combined garage and stable. No, too much activity there. The greenhouse was a much better, more secluded, spot.

They had one last night to explore. It had to be the greenhouse. The distance from the house, coupled with the silence between the two, should make their night foray just a tad easier. Lynn had no idea what they might find, if anything, but Alfred knew more than a gentleman's share about gardening sheds and such. She was confident he would know the nooks and crannies to explore. She would do everything she could to support him.

"Come into my bower!" Alain called, holding open the door to the greenhouse.

Lynn had been dawdling, but at his call, she hustled to join Alfred at the threshold.

The greenhouse interior stretched out before them. Lynn could see the glass wall at the far end. The central aisle was clean of debris and bracketed by waist-high tables packed with plants, like wedding guests in a full church. Under the tables, clay pots and hand gardening tools lay in random piles and groups, separated by empty grow trays and bags of... Lynn wasn't sure what everything was, but she recognized the smell of packaged manure. Alfred would have called it "fragrance," as if it were imported perfume from France. She never saw the attraction of it, but did have to concede that Alfred grew the most glorious flowers and vegetables because of it.

She returned her attention to Alain, who was leading them deeper into the greenhouse. Looking at the glass panels that made up the ceiling, she elicited Alain's comment.

"Don't mind the wind," he said. "The panes are quite sturdy." He pointed at the roof ridge. "See those louvers up there? They are regulated by oil."

"Really!" Alfred's gardening muse made an appearance. "So, the louvers open and close depending on the temperature."

Alain nodded. "Right. Warm weather and the oil expands, which activates the mechanisms to open the louvers. Cold nights? The louvers close. Perfect solution to keeping the temperature and humidity under control."

"Wondrous. I simply must get myself a greenhouse. Can you give me the address of the manufacturer, please? Once this war is over–"

Lynn returned Alfred's earlier gesture of the firm grip on the arm. "Oh, darling, I'd like to know about some of the flowers here. You two can talk shop later."

He apparently got the message, as he patted her hand delivering its death grip. "You're right. I get carried away sometimes when it comes to gardening. I'm really just a farmer who happens to act."

That sent Alain into deep guffaws. "No one on this earth would ever consider you a farmer first." He clapped Alfred on the shoulder. "But come, let me show you some of our prizes here."

The three of them set off down the aisle, Alain pointing out ferns and bedding plants. An occasional climbing vine, or small tree-like plant, provided variety among the usual geraniums and other fauna packed into containers, waiting to be transplanted around the estate outdoors.

Lynn stopped at one particular vine that took up a great deal of space as it reached out and up. White blossoms proliferated along the stems, but they were all tightly curled, as if protecting some precious nectar inside. "What are these, Alain? They're beautiful." She corrected herself. "Well, they would be beautiful if they were open. They do open, don't they?"

"Yes, they do. And you're right, they are gorgeous. Those are moonflowers, and they open only at night." He spread his fingers as wide as they would go. "Like this, like saucers or dinner plates."

"Hence, the name," Lynn said. "Moonflowers. Open when the moon is out." A thought struck her like an earthquake in her mind. She struggled to keep from rushing to Alfred and blurting out the importance of these innocent flowers. She tucked her brainstorm into a vacant corner to share later.

Overlapping her effort was the sudden appearance of a portion of the greenhouse floor tipping up a few steps in front of them. She grabbed Alfred's hand for balance.

"What?" Alfred's question wasn't directed at her, but at the rising square of floor, tilting in front of them.

Alain seemed unconcerned as the trapdoor-for that is what it was-continued to rise. A head appeared over the edge.

"Lord Bufort. Didn't expect you."

"Lynn, Alfred, meet my head gardener, William." Alain finished the introductions as William emerged completely from below and lowered the trapdoor into place again. He wiped his hands down his thighs before offering a handshake to Alfred, and a bow of the head to Lynn. "Don't let us keep you, Will. I know you're in the midst of work here."

William sent a quick obeisance to his employer, nodded at the Lunts and turned to lope into the distant regions of the greenhouse.

"Pretty taciturn," Alfred said, not without humor.

"Never one to waste words when actions speak louder," Alain said. "A hard worker, and an even better gardener. Worth his weight in gold, that one is."

Lynn thought of the people hired to work the land and tend to the house back home at Ten Chimneys. A moment of nostalgia for peacetime in their haven in Wisconsin. Before that became painful, she brought herself to bear on the present. "The good ones are."

Alain was extolling the value of a full basement, even in a greenhouse. He explained that the mechanisms for pumping irrigation water up to the plants was all down there. "Not many people have a full basement in an outbuilding, but it's made William's work so much easier. I was happy to take him up on his suggestion when we built this."

"We have the same thing at our poolhouse back home," Alfred said. "Water readily available."

Lynn saw the glint in his eye that told her he had more on his mind than his own poolhouse. She relaxed a bit, having ascertained that perhaps he was seeing the same thing she did. She could hardly wait to get back to the Old Manor to closet themselves in and plan strategy.

After a thorough tour of the greenhouse, Alain led them back up the lawn at a leisurely stroll. He and Alfred talked incessantly of seeds, soils, fertilizers, the advantages of this tool over that, the best way to coax difficult or diseased plants into giving their all. Their chatter made Lynn's head spin.

Never one to rise early just to see the sun come up over a sleepy garden at Ten Chimneys, Lynn much preferred to lie abed until the shafts of light crept over the sill and tiptoed across her blanket. On bright days, that was enough of an invitation for her to at least think about getting up to begin the day. On dreary days, it was more of an effort. Usually, the aroma of Alfred's coffee winding its way up the stairs was sufficient to get her moving. But only because of Alfred in the kitchen, not because of the coffee. She was a confirmed tea drinker. Which Alfred knew full well. She knew he had a pot of Earl Grey steeping under a cozy, the pot's own blanket to match her own. Usually, she burrowed down under the covers before a grand foray to greet the day. That meant a dash for the bathroom before wrapping in a home-sewn dressing gown appropriate to the season.

Oh, how she missed Ten Chimneys! Even walking here, across the impossibly green grass and looking over her shoulder at the wisps of clouds over the Channel, Lynn could be transported back to their beloved summer home. One of these days... Which may stretch into years, if the war would continue.

That brought her up short. She realized she was dawdling again. The men were far ahead of her, almost to the terrace. This was a perfect moment to regroup mentally. She and Alfred had a job here: find out how Lord Bufort planned to help the Reich. It was clear to her that the Quartet was not simply a group of innocuous guests. The Alsatian accent, coupled with the glimpse of the Nazi eagle on the cigarette case made it clear for her. Those men were here to plan...what? Bufort's estate was on the coast. Yes, she told herself, but the cliffs here were too steep, with little to no beach, for a force of any size to land and invade. But that didn't preclude landing a small party of four.

How had the Quartet arrived here, anyway? She trolled her memories. Alain said they came by train. It didn't really matter how they got there, did it? Only that they were here. Here to plan and execute some plan of the Reich to bring England to its knees and cut its head off.

She shivered. A thought too horrible to contemplate. Her reasonable side asserted itself. From what they heard through the news and from rumors, the Germans were getting desperate. The number of U-boats that plagued the Channel and the Atlantic seemed to be diminished, even considering Alfred's and her own encounter on the high seas on their way to Portugal. Coupled with that, the RAF was doing a crackerjack job of protecting the English skies and penetrating German-held lands, even flying deeper into Germany itself. Power stations, harbors, research facilities, industrial complexes, and more, were pounded by RAF, US, and Canadian bombers. Was that enough to actually turn the tide?

Somehow, the Allies needed to get onto the Continent in greater numbers. As the weather emerged from unpredictable spring, perhaps summer would provide opportunities that the winter of early 1944 could not. Lynn sighed. They were already deep into May. She hoped for favorable weather. She hoped for an Allied landing in Europe, not a German one coming up across the Channel to the beaches of southeastern England. She hoped most of all for solid useful information for James Hamilton.

She had a plan in mind. She set off at a lope across the lawn to catch up to the men.

-23-

Teatime passed, and the Lunts repaired to their room to talk about Lynn's plan. It turned out that Alfred was already on the same page.

They stretched out on the bed, having first checked for evidence of disturbance in the room, as they did every single time they walked in, whether to discuss strategy or to simply take a nap.

"We have to get into that greenhouse, Alfred," Lynn said. "That basement is a perfect place for a clandestine meeting. I don't know how big it is, but even if it's only as wide as the greenhouse above it, there should be plenty of room for the Quartet and Alain."

"Plus a table for planning or maps or...whatever," Alfred said, tucking his hands behind his head and staring at the ceiling. "Our poolhouse isn't anywhere near the size of Alain's greenhouse, and there's plenty of room for our caretaker, me, and all the equipment for pumping water."

"I have an idea," Lynn said.

But Alfred was off in his own world, listing the things that could be secreted in Alain's greenhouse basement.

"Alfred!" Lynn poked her husband in the ribs.

He rotated his head to face her. "Did I miss something? Sorry, Lynnie. I'm just worried about how we're going to get down there. We'll go after dark, of course. There is a generous quarter moon, so–"

Lynn rolled to her side to face Alfred and set a hand gently over his mouth. "Just listen, Alfred. I have a plan."

Alfred nodded and Lynn took her hand away. She propped herself up onto her elbow. "It's easy, Alfred. We can go back after dark to see the moonflower blossoms open." She waited, knowing he would see the value of that.

His response was an instantaneous, "Grand! You are, as I've always known, a genius, my dear." He leaned toward her and blew her a kiss. "Even if someone sees us from the house, that is a very plausible explanation."

Lynn smiled. "I'm surprised you didn't think of that yourself."

"Well, I must admit, I was quite taken with the greenhouse itself. The flowers rather took a backseat to my farmer instincts." He raised himself up on an elbow to face her.

Lynn smiled. "That's why we make such a good team. It's so easy to see the direction the other person is headed. Not that we don't argue..." They did, but arguments mostly devolved into productive discussions. Unless he tried to direct her too much on stage movements. Then she rebelled.

She cleared her mind. A tale for another day.

"Time for a nap, Lynnie," Alfred said, ignoring her comment about arguing. "We need all of our senses sharp, if we're going to do this right."

"Agreed," Lynn said. "I hope we can make it through dinner without giving ourselves away."

"We are consummate actors, my darling girl," Alfred said, flopping back down. "We can do anything we set our minds to."

Lynn turned away and scooched backwards, the better to fit herself into the curve of Alfred's side. "So our fans tell us. Time to put it to the test."

Alfred's breathing was already deep and even.

In spite of her excitement and apprehension, Lynn fell into a deep sleep within a few minutes, curled tight against her husband, as if to draw strength from their union.

The centerpieces of dinner were pork roast and small potatoes, both raised and grown locally. The fragrance of those, along with that of buttered vegetables and fresh bread, was almost lost on Lynn, focused as she was on the plan to raid the greenhouse later in the night.

Almost, but not quite. She was the beneficiary of Alfred's generous cooking, and learned the lesson early on to especially compliment his vegetables, all homegrown. As his mother always warned, "If you don't rhapsodize over even his vegetables, all evening he will be in a blue funk."

She realigned her focus, not wanting to be caught losing out on what might be important conversation. She also didn't want to project the image of a fully ditzy female. A touch or two was fine, but beyond that, she wouldn't intentionally destroy her sterling reputation. Only dent it a bit.

In spite of that, for the most part, Lynn sat back and let Alfred lead the pack. She forced herself to eat slowly and deliberately, murmuring compliments on the food. The conversations ebbed and flowed, and turned out to be nothing of consequence. She felt Alain gently manipulating topics, keeping everything light and airy. At first, when they were all seated, Alain said, "No talk of war or bombs or fear tonight. Let's make this last meal for the Lunts a positive affair."

The wording "last meal" set Lynn's hair to stand on end, or at least feel that way. Enough so that she reached up to smooth any electrified strands back in place. Hopefully, this was not a prophecy for their skullduggery later.

Later finally came, after a long after-dinner stop in the library for brandy and cigars, which Alfred eschewed. He and Lynn preferred to indulge in small glasses of sherry, both of which remained unfinished by the time all of them set off for bed at midnight.

Everyone shuffled off upstairs, stopping briefly on the landing to Alain's quarters to exchange one more bit of polite conversation. On the pretense of retying a shoe, Alfred hung back. The soft sound of Alain's door opening and closing satisfied them. Lynn, usually fully disciplined from work on the stage, felt herself unraveling. The remainder of the party, including Lynn and Alfred, continued on to the guest bedrooms.

When she and Alfred reached their room, she sent a last scintillating smile to those going on to their own rooms. Lynn and Alfred stepped into their bedroom, leaving the door ajar a mere crack, then turned into statues, listening to see if they could detect any sounds from the others. Only the muffled creakings of doors closing. They counted. All guests safely tucked away. Even Alain.

Alfred watched at the door while Lynn pulled out clothes more appropriate than dinner jacket for him and pearls for her. They dressed quickly and silently in dark tweed pants, topped by charcoal-grey sweaters. She rummaged around in the stack of riding clothes used earlier in their visit and came up with leather gloves. Alfred lifted two chairs into place in front of the window overlooking the courtyard and sat down to pull on heavy socks.

Lynn joined him and set a hand on his knee. "How late do you think we should wait?" Her whisper barely carried.

"I'd say about two hours," Alfred whispered back.

She raised one eyebrow, but didn't comment. He was the one who prowled around in the semi-dark at home, looking over his fencing to make sure the deer hadn't broken into his garden. Or took himself for a short stroll to clear his head after a New York performance. She trusted his judgment on that front. She herself preferred the indoors when the sun took itself down below the horizon. Now, she settled in for the long wait.

Lynn was nudged out of a hazy doze. "Dark and quiet, Lynnie. Time to make our move," Alfred whispered in her ear.

That brought her fully awake. "No shoes, Alfred. We'll need the Wellies. We can get jackets in the mudroom too. Carrying ours would be too suspicious."

He nodded. "Should be no problem to get downstairs and into the other wing. We could have lots of reasons for prowling around downstairs. Once we're outside, we'll have to stick to the shadows as much as possible."

They needed no excuses, however, as they met no one when they crept through the house. They found the Wellies and pulled them on. Even the back door gave no resistance or sound as they stepped out onto the grass.

With every corner and moonwashed stretch, they stopped, reconnoitered, then streaked like wraiths for the dark. Once along the woodline, they rushed along, passing the path to the folly. The moon cooperated by seeming to avoid the few clouds in the sky. The light was just enough to allow Alfred, followed step for step by Lynn, to make their way quickly to the greenhouse.

The glass panes reflected the night sky and the moon. No light shone inside the greenhouse. They waited. Lynn held her breath, Alfred marble beside her.

In the pale light, they exchanged glances. Lynn raised her eyebrows in inquiry, even though she knew it was unlikely Alfred could see that.

Perhaps he did, as faced the door and slowly, ever so slowly, turned the handle to the greenhouse. It made not a sound. Alfred opened the door, shifting into slow-motion. Still no sound.

They slipped inside and, Alfred in the lead, started down the central aisle. Though the greenhouse appeared empty, Lynn knew they dare not chance noise. Who knew what had been–or perhaps still was–going on.

When they reached the moonflower, Alfred held up a hand to stop. The trapdoor in the floor was directly in front of them. In the moonlight coming through the glass ceiling, Alfred was visible. He looked back at Lynn and touched his ear.

She returned the gesture and nodded, knowing he must have heard something. Perhaps it was only a mouse. But...perhaps not.

She locked her gaze on the moonflowers, their buds now opened into glorious blossoms. Letting her eyes lose their focus a bit, she concentrated on sound. Yes, mumblings were coming from beneath the floor. She set her hand on Alfred's shoulder to let him know she was attuned to him.

Alfred settled into a squat and leaned forward, cocking his head in the age-old gesture of close listening. He held up his hand again. A request for total silence.

Lynn took only shallow breaths and didn't move to join Alfred. He would have to listen for both of them. She caught only bits and pieces: "coast...south...France...RAF..." Little else. She hoped Alfred could piece more together.

The voices shifted in tone. A bit louder, hardly noticeable.

Alfred stood up and put a finger on his lips. He took a half-step toward her.

Lynn saw the edge of the trapdoor lift away from the floor.

She grabbed Alfred's arm. A split second...

She let out with a piercing scream worthy of the finest horror film.

-24-

Chaos ensued.

Lynn's scream modulated like an air raid siren.

"Are you-" Alfred. "What the h-" Alain. "Why is she-" One of the Quartet. "Can't we-" "How much did-" "-all right?" "-finish-" "-save our papers!"

Lynn went from screams to great sobbing gulps, as noisy as she could produce, enhanced by a small flood of tears. "Help me, Alfred!" She squeezed out a phrase now and then, timed to drown out Alain's questions. Even pressed up against Alfred's chest, she managed to maneuver into position to peer out and see, with one eye, those emerging from the open trapdoor. Alain. One of the Quartet. Then the second, the Alsatian, who carried a sheaf of papers clutched in one hand while he used the other to balance himself as he clambered up and out.

Without a second's thought, she drove against Alfred, who stumbled against the trapdoor. He threw out an arm to catch himself, pushing on the trapdoor as he fell. The Alsatian fell forward, clear of the door as it fell, papers scattering from his hands.

"Oh! Oh! Oh!" Lynn's renewed shriek drew everyone's momentary attention to her. She fervently hoped Alfred had a chance to grab at least one of those papers as they fluttered and scattered. She plastered her hands to her face and waded into the fray. "Oh! Oh! Are you all right?" She reached Alain, the man closest to her. "You scared the wits out of me! What are you doing here?" Better to get the question in first, before Alain had a chance to regroup and ask her the same thing. And best to answer first as well. "We came down to see the moonflowers open." She grabbed his arm and spun him to look toward the moonflower vine.

"What am *I* doing here?" Alain was clearly a fraction behind the time, before realizing Lynn already answered the next question he could ask.

Alfred rushed to Lynn's side and enveloped her in a protective embrace. She let go of Alain's arm to curl into her husband. "Lynn woke me up all excited. She could see the moon shining through our window, and said she simply had to come down to see the flowers open. It's our last night, she said, if we didn't come now, we might never get back..."

He continued along that line, Lynn recognizing his well-played ploy to run off at the mouth. Her heartrate slowed, returning closer to normal, but she continued to breathe heavily to maintain what she set up.

Alfred was bumbling along with multiple apologies, some of them rather flowery, all of them designed to stymie the listener. He wound down at last, with a final, "We never meant to cause you trouble, Alain."

By this time, Alain pulled himself together. He took a very deep breath. "I think you scared me as much as I scared you." He turned to the two Quartets and motioned them toward the door. "Many thanks for helping me stop that leak. My poor plants would be dead by morning if they flooded. And William would have my head." Alain seemed all solicitous toward the Lunts.

The two Quartet members murmured a response and took their leave, pile of papers clutched tightly to one's chest.

Lynn and Alfred were left facing Alain. What would be his reaction?

Lynn controlled a natural flinch as Alain reached over her shoulder. "Here. They are beautiful." He plucked an open moonflower blossom and slid it into her hair over her ear. "I should've thought to offer to bring you down here tonight. It may be, after all, as you said, your last chance to see them open."

Lynn heard what she thought was the threat behind the words, though Alain's tone of voice belied no such thing. She pasted on her best smile. "I'm so sorry we startled you. We had no idea you were having trouble with your indoor irrigation system, or we never would have come down. So, so sorry for our imposition." She leaned over and patted him on the chest.

Alain returned her smile. It appeared to be genuine, not a devious grin. "It gave us all quite a fright."

I'll bet it did, Lynn thought, though her face betrayed only dismay at inconveniencing their host.

"Come." Alain turned them to the green house door and directed them out. "Let's get you two back to the Old Manor, now that we've had our excitement for the night. I hope you were impressed with my moonflowers. They are spectacular when open, don't you think?"

The walk back to the house was filled with compliments on the night-blooming flowers, delighted exclamations on the phases of the moon, observations of the effect of moonlight on the trees and grass. Anything to deflect interest from the Lunts' nocturnal excursion into what was clearly forbidden territory. Lynn observed Alain closely, becoming more and more convinced as they approached the Old Manor, that the lord's suspicion of them was sloughing away as they walked, their conversation was so ordinary, so banal. Their performances, though frustratingly unrehearsed, seemed to have taken hold.

Thank you, Alfred, for your ability to lie, Lynn breathed silently. He often created false birthdates for himself, invented names and places that were totally foreign to him. He never even produced autographs with his real signature, having discovered that someone tried to counterfeit his real signature on a check. This served them both well, but, Lynn thought, was sure to boggle the mind of anyone doing research on them in the future. But for the present moment, she was glad of his inventive mind.

Once back in the Old Manor, and tucked safely into bed, Lynn wanted to question her husband as to what he found, what he heard, but he put a finger to his lips in a gesture of silence.

Once in his pajamas, Alfred pulled a crumpled piece of paper from the back pocket of the pants hanging over the chair where he put them. He set the paper on the bed, and skated his fingers across to smooth out the worst wrinkles. Lynn assumed it was a scrap that flew out of one of the Quartet's hands as he scrambled around in the greenhouse.

Alfred knelt down next to the bed and hunched over the paper, eyebrows almost meeting over his nose as he tried to read. "Grabbed this while you distracted everyone." Lynn sat up and crawled across to join him. He leaned close enough to Lynn so she could feel his breath on her ear as he whispered, "Numbers. No idea what they mean."

Lynn squinted, looked this way and that at the paper, then shook her head in agreement. Rather than say anything, she turned her hands palms up. She too had no idea what the rows of numbers meant. Some rows were shorter than others, some had numerals missing. None of it made any sense.

Alfred folded up the paper, lifted up the edge of the mattress and tucked the paper under, doing his best to keep it flat. He crawled into bed and positioned the pillows, pummeling until they formed a soft backstop so he was propped against the headboard.

Lynn fused herself to his side, then stretched up to whisper, "What did you hear, Alfred? I could tell you heard something before Alain made that dramatic entrance."

"Something about massive German troop movements in Calais." He frowned. "Something about Folkestone, but I couldn't hear what. What did you hear?"

"Not much more than you did." She told him of the fragments she caught. "Anything else?"

"I don't think so, but that trapdoor rattled me. I need to go over everything." Alfred closed his eyes, and his lips began to move.

Lynn recognized his personal rehearsal technique, and fell silent, so as not to break into his concentration. She stretched over him and turned out the light. If she didn't disturb his ruminations now, by morning, his lines would be firmly and precisely in place. Everything he heard or saw in the greenhouse would be memorized and placed in a mental folder, to be revealed probably on the train to London the next morning. She realized his need for silence. Time enough for sharing when they were safely away.

However, in the morning, their best laid plans gang agley, as Bobbie Burns put it way back in the 1700s.

"I'm heading back to London today myself," Alain said, spreading marmalade on his toast. "My friends had to leave very early this morning, so I have no reason to play the host to an empty house. Without you two here as well, I'd be all alone, and far from all the fun in London. So..." He sent a smile across the table.

Lynn mentally cringed. The Quartet was gone. Something was afoot. Would she and Alfred be able to get their information back to Hamilton before...something...happened? She finished her slow sip of tea and turned her attention back to Alain. This was no time to allow her mind to wander.

"So?" Alfred said. He sat with a forkful of omelet hovering over the plate.

"No need to take the train, old man," Alain said. "You can ride back to the city with me." His tone rose in a perfect complement to the glow on his face. "Won't that be wonderful? We'll get you back to London in comfort. Certainly better than the train." He cocked his head, surely waiting for a matching excitement from the Lunts.

Alfred clearly read the signs. "That is terrific. I wasn't looking forward to the bumpy ride, to say nothing of the unpleasant smell of a diesel-fired engine." He returned his attention to attacking the rest of his breakfast.

Lynn took the baton. "That is so generous of you, Alain. Alfred's right. This will be so much more comfortable."

"We can discuss your coming appearances," Alain said. "I can't wait to see you ensconced back in the Aldwych."

Lynn was reluctant to share anything with this man, but she was a good enough actress to hide all that. She clapped her hands, then rose from the chair. "I'm going up and make sure I've packed everything. Come and help me carry my bags down, Alfred." The least she could do was rescue him from further stress and strain. The chances were nil that he would forget and utter something he shouldn't, but she would rather not leave him alone with Alain. Nerves. Never a good thing when so much hung in the balance.

-25-

The ride back to London was long and winding, to use a cliché. Alain insisted on joining them in the back seat of the Bentley, behind the chauffeur, so as to better continue the conversation with Alfred, begun as they walked to the car. Though the men had diverse interests, one dear to both of them was clearly gardening. When the chauffeur opened the rear door, Lynn insisted on riding next to a window, leaving Alfred shoulder to shoulder with her, and Alain buttressing him on the other side. Without involving Lynn, the two men were free to discuss the merits of various strains of flowers and vegetables, as well as the value of overwintering green horse manure for use in the spring garden.

"I've always delighted in the German word for manure," Alain said. "Mist. It sounds so much more cultured, don't you think?"

That was one of the few lines that aroused Lynn from her passivity. The word "German" caused her ears to prick up, though she realized the remainder of the conversation was banal, and she sank back into what looked like bored lethargy. In reality, she was listening with care to everything that came out of Alain's mouth. She was disappointed for much of the trip, as the two men went from rhapsodizing to practicality, and back again.

While the trip should take three hours or less, depending on road traffic and conditions, Lynn checked her watch at the two-hour mark, and realized they were not following the usual routes. Not wanting to draw the men away from their conversations, and knowing Alfred was every bit as alert as he could be to what Alain was saying, Lynn turned her attention to the surrounding fields and roads. She sat, chin in hand, and stared out the window, allowing only her eyes to scan the sights. What she saw was enlightening. Behind hedgerows stood farmsteads and fields with military equipment, mainly trucks, tucked away as if waiting for something, drivers perhaps, or petrol. With a more discerning glance, Lynn could see movements, flashes, glimpses. Were those troops? More equipment? As they reached one small village after another, she realized that these were no longer the steady, methodical movements of daily replenishments. These were heavy pieces in clusters larger than she saw before. Also, every train they passed was filled to the brim with soldiers, soldiers clearly on their way to war, with helmets, rifles, bayonets, monstrous packs. The more she looked, the more details she garnered.

This May, May 1944, was one of the hottest on record. A perfect time for skirmishes or invasions, with heat, not rain, providing decent road conditions.

She sneaked a glance at Alain, but he seemed deep in conversation with Alfred. She sensed Alfred's tense leg against hers, and knew he saw what she did, and was doing his best to keep Lord Bufort busy. Anything to serve as a diversion. However, the chauffeur was scanning the road ahead, as well as the surroundings. Lynn didn't notice any reduction of speed, unless there was a good reason for it, but from his shoulders lifting, and his head sweeping back and forth, she knew he was quite aware of what was going on out there.

Troops and materiel heading for...where? Mostly going south, by the looks of it. South to the coast. That made a jarring intersection with what she and Alfred were carrying in their memories of the conversations at Forest Hall, inadvertently overheard by the implanted SOE spies...them.

Lynn shivered, then tamped down any outward sign of her concern. They had to reach London and report what they knew to James Hamilton. From the looks of it, Allies might be headed across the Channel waters. Or perhaps it was all an attempt to confront a German invasion. She wondered if all the movements she was seeing were just as easily seen by the Germans barricaded along the opposite coast. How could they not be? Considering the high heat and generally good forecasts for this end of May, the weather did seem to favor some kind of offensive against the Germans. Or a German offensive against England. Were the Germans thinking of a preemptive run to the English coast while the weather was so good? She herself heard words and broken phrases, saw pieces of a coastal map back at Forest Hall, that seemed to point in that direction.

She was frustrated, unable to trawl Alfred's memories because of Alain's interference with their train travel plans. How much information were they carrying that would be true? Or useful? What was in that envelope? What else was going on that they didn't know about? Whatever the intelligence, it was imperative they must, with all speed, report.

She shifted with impatience. How close was London? And would Hamilton be accessible once they got there?

Shading her eyes, she peered around the chauffeur's shoulder to focus out the front windscreen. At last, the ragged outline of the city appeared against the gray sky hovering over London. So much damage, thanks to the Luftwaffe, rendered many of the familiar, and beloved, spires, domes, and chimneys almost unrecognizable. The city, still proud, raised defiant fingers of broken buildings to their attackers. Lynn watched in silence as they drew closer and closer. Walls standing alone, like Hollywood movie sets, stretched upward, some of them exposing living quarters ravaged by the bombs. Bathtubs hung precariously, closets with doors blown off showed clothing still hanging in neat rows. When Lynn saw a children's nursery with toys and books plastered to the wall from the force of the explosions, she turned her gaze to her hands clasped in her lap. Even with that, she couldn't see clearly through the haze of tears.

Lynn took a deep breath and hardened her lips into a tight line. She was beginning to feel desperate. The Germans must be stopped, stopped at all costs. If she and Alfred had a part to play, no matter how small the role, then they must step up, and as soon as possible. Who knew the true value of what they had to offer?

She interrupted the men, who were immersed in tomato talk. "Alain, we seem to have taken the long way around." To cement her rather vapid mindset, she added, "Was that way more scenic?"

"What? Oh, yes, we planned the back roads for just that reason," Alain said.

I doubt that, Lynn thought. *More likely, it gave your driver a chance to take in any new troop movements. One more thing to report to James.* "How lovely." She gave Alfred's leg a soft nudge.

He launched into one of his diversionary monologues. "It *was* lovely. At least, I think it was lovely going that way. We were so busy talking vegetables that I didn't notice much along the way though. Right, Alain? I'll bet you didn't even think about where we were, considering you make the trip so often." Alfred's tone shifted from apologetic to conspiratorial as he massaged Alain into revealing whether or not he actually was watching the scenery.

Alain laughed. "You're right, Alfred. I don't always pay much attention to the hedges and fields. We're back and forth regularly, so I leave everything to my servant."

That confirmed Lynn's suspicions. Alain shifted gears between Forest Hall and London, leaving much of the physical transition and its alterations across the kilometers to his minions.

Minions. Lynn caught herself in a rare tone of repulsion, or perhaps even disgust, at the lord's attitude toward his those who served him. She was cautious with Alain before, heeding Hamilton's warning not to take him lightly, as he seemed to easily deceive others with a hail-and-well-met surface that concealed a suspected Nazi sympathizer. The veil slipped infrequently, but when it did, the powers that be pegged him as not just a sympathizer, but a collaborator. That was what she and Alfred were commissioned to help determine.

Determine it, they did. The coastal map from Alain's study, the mumbled conversations, especially what Alfred heard in the greenhouse, all of those pretty well confirmed their suspicions.

Feeling like a petulant two-year old, she said, "Are we almost there?", then clamped her jaw shut, lest it betray her nervous impatience. They would get there when they got there, no sooner, no later. She forced her foot not to tap-tap-tap against the floor mat.

Alfred patted her knee. "Almost, darling."

Alain leaned across Alfred. "We can have lunch at your hotel, Lynn, before I go on to my digs. A final hurrah, so to speak."

I'd rather have lunch with the Savoy's black cat, Lynn thought. She suppressed a smile at the thought of the carving, waiting serenely back at the hotel. Superstition ruled it *verboten* to have thirteen at table, especially after one of the...lords, was it? An illustrious guest flaunted the superstition and suffered a hideous death after being the first person to leave the table with thirteen diners. Since then, the cat, complete with linen napkin tied around its neck and served every course, presided when a fourteenth guest was needed.

Alfred was talking. "I'm sorry we can't lunch with you, old man. "We simply must come down from the clouds and prepare for our next performances."

Lynn glanced at Alain, almost prepared to see whiskers and enigmatic cat's eyes. But no. Thank the stars for that. "But we had a wonderful holiday with you at Forest Hall. What a delightful home you have, and so very restful." All of that a remaking of the truth. "Perhaps lunch some other time, however?"

"Whenever you wish," Alain said. "Ah! The city at last."

Lynn turned to the window.

They motored into London proper, but the condition of the roads and the precarious pieces of bombed out buildings had them weaving through this street and that before they finally pulled up to the familiar façade of the Savoy, serene and in one piece. Mostly. Some of the windows were still boarded up, but the bustle of guests and others at ground level belied the damage behind them.

While the chauffeur unloaded their luggage, Lynn and Alfred emerged from the car and went into the expected raptures and gratitudes that they knew would please Lord Bufort. They saw him back in the Bentley and waved him goodbye before turning in a measured pace to enter the lobby.

Lynn took a quick look to ensure that Kaspar, the black cat sculpture, was indeed still awaiting his call at the reception desk, then joined Alfred in the lift with their luggage. She relaxed enough to smile, but didn't trust herself to say a word. If they waited this long to hold their secrets, they could defer just a bit longer.

The bellhop took their bags into the entryway of the suite and stepped aside for Lynn and Alfred before disappearing out the door, closing it behind him.

Lynn kicked off her shoes and, walking backwards, moved into the living room. "I'm about to burst, Alfred, if–"

"So am I!" James Hamilton's voice rang out behind her.

She spun around to see James poised with a teapot, ready to pour. Her heart started to regain its normal rhythm.

Alfred was laughing. "I saw him sitting there, just before you nearly collapsed." He thrust out his hand and walked to Hamilton. "Welcome."

"I should be saying the same to you," James said. "But I can see you are about to burst, as Lynn said." He set down the teapot and grew serious. "This can wait. Sit and tell me what you found."

-26-

Lynn picked up the coat she dropped when Hamilton surprised her and tossed it on the hall tree. "Give him the camera, Alfred." An entirely unnecessary comment, as Alfred was already handing over the little camera he kept stowed in an inner pocket. She shook her head at herself. Of course, he was on top of things. She joined the men, planting herself in one of the chairs across from Alfred and James on the couch. The tea set sat placid on the table between the men and Lynn's chair, the teapot once more keeping warm under its cozy. She settled back, satisfied with letting Alfred take the bit in his mouth first.

"Did you find anything?" James bent over and retrieved a notebook and pencil from his briefcase sitting on the floor, then settled back, ready to write. He asked no probing questions beyond that simple first one. "Don't worry. Your suite is safe."

Such patience. If it were her, Lynn would be exploding with questions. Was already. But of course, that could easily disrupt any ordered thoughts Alfred had for giving out information. Unfortunately, Lynn and Alfred were not able to debrief and rehearse before Lord Bufort's untimely intrusion into their plans. She set her elbows on the chair arms and tented her fingers in front of her mouth. When Alfred glanced at her, she sent him a tiny nod that said, "You first, darling."

Alfred swung his attention to James. "Did we find anything. Oh, yes, yes, we did. First, get the film from that camera developed, and you'll find a map of part of the English coast, a bit south and east of Bufort's estate."

Lynn took note of the lack of title for Alain. Gone were the social niceties.

"At least," Alfred said, "I hope we caught it. We were able to get into his study."

James sat up straight and flattened one hand on the brocade of the couch. "How on earth did you manage that? We couldn't get anyone near the house, much less into his private study."

Lynn laughed. "I became suddenly faint, and it was the closest door. Wasn't that such a lovely coincidence?"

Hamilton shook his head. "Leave it to actors. Well done." He waved his pencil at them. "Go on."

Alfred took over. "Someone drew lines on the map, lines–arrows maybe–that came from the east, France, most likely."

"A corner was torn off the paper, but we could see part of a swastika left behind," Lynn said. "Unfortunately, we weren't able to get to any other papers, because we heard Bufort and others headed our way in the corridor."

"That's where Lynn's acting skills came into play," Alfred said, "saving the day by that clever diversion. We think he bought it, but we really doubled down on taking care from then on."

James tsked. "Too bad you couldn't get more. But that map–"

Lynn interrupted. "Oh, no. That's not all. Give him the envelope, Alfred."

"Ah, yes. I almost forgot." Alfred stood and fumbled at his waist to release the money belt. He pulled it loose and took out the envelope, handing it off to Hamilton. "No idea what's in it."

"We thought it best to save it for you," Lynn said. "It was under a couch in Alain's study, so it may be no more than a lost birthday card."

James levered a finger under the flap and pulled out a piece of thin onion-skin paper. As he scanned the sheet, his face went from bland to taut to open-mouthed amazement. He held up the paper with two fingers, as if it were a lover's silk handkerchief. "I don't believe it. I..."

Lynn and Alfred exchanged a perplexed glance. "Is it worth something?" Alfred asked.

"What? Worth?" James seemed caught speechless. "Oh, yes, yes, indeed." He frowned.

Lynn rescued him. "Please, don't feel you need to tell us."

James folded the paper and put it back in the envelope with care. "I...You're entitled to know something, at least." He cleared his throat. "It is a...well, it's in code, which we'll have to decipher. But something tells me it's speculation on where Allied forces might land in France."

So, there is to be an invasion, Lynn thought. She waited for James to give them what he could.

"That's about all I can say, but this is paper and envelope that can be traced to...our side," James said. "Where did you find this?"

"Under a couch in Bufort's study," Alfred said, "as we told you."

"Sorry, I was just flummoxed by this. Do you think it was put there deliberately, or dropped and somehow kicked under the couch?"

"I'd say the latter," Alfred said. "Wouldn't you agree, Lynnie? After all, he never detained us, or somehow or other gave anything overt or covert that he suspected us of finding it."

"I think you're right, Alfred," Lynn said. "And if he hid it deliberately, he clearly didn't check before we all left for London. I believe he may not have known it was delivered. Perhaps he's still looking for delivery."

"Well, it really doesn't matter now," James said. "We've got it, and they don't. That was probably their last attempt to find out where...any invasion from England would land. It's no secret that we're mobilizing. No way to hide that. The big thing is where and when."

"We can assume that this note said where, if not when." Alfred was not posing a question.

Hamilton sat silent.

Which gave Lynn the only answer she required. She remembered there was more that they discovered. "Tell him about the Quartet and the greenhouse, Alfred." She sat back to watch her husband retrieve his well-rehearsed thoughts from that nighttime foray.

Alfred filled Hamilton in on their reconnaissance of the greenhouse, including the fortuitous excuse of wanting to see the open blossoms of the moonflowers, and Lynn's ear-shattering scream that helped cover up Bufort's suspicions of the two interlopers.

Lynn pulled out the scrap of paper dropped by one of the Quartet and squirreled away by Alfred. She handed it over to James. "We couldn't figure out what these rows of number are all about. Maybe you can make more sense out of it."

They waited patiently, watching Hamilton's frown deepen more and more as he looked over the scribblings.

"It's hard to tell, but some of the numbers might correspond to military detachments. I'm sure our experts can figure out more." He tucked the paper into his briefcase.

"What's this 'Quartet' you mentioned?" His fingers made little quotation marks in the air.

"Just a nickname we gave them," Lynn said. "Four of them, guests of Bufort. But they never really mingled. We wondered from the beginning, but our suspicions were confirmed over time. Two of them rarely talked, much less with us, but they were clearly British. The others..." She settled back in her chair, a sign for Alfred to take over.

Alfred told Hamilton of the man who claimed to be a Parisian, but spoke with an Alsatian accent, putting him close to Germany, not Paris. Lynn added the detail of the cigarette case with the Nazi eagle.

"We're aware of English friends of Bufort, but the other two..." James held his hands out in a show of ignorance. "There's little information we can find about them."

"German, for sure," Alfred said. "Lynn caught that."

"Tell James what you heard in the greenhouse. You heard a lot more than I did. I only heard something about the south coast, barges, and the RAF."

Alfred said, "I hope I heard something useful, but they were in the basement of the greenhouse, under a closed trapdoor."

Hamilton raised both eyebrows, but waited for Alfred to continue.

Alfred tented his fingers in front of his lips and closed his eyes. "I did hear 'along the south coast near Folkstone.'"

James slid to the front of his chair and set his hands on his knees.

"Something about barges, though I couldn't tell what they meant." Alfred opened his eyes. "I hope I heard right."

"So do I," James said. "We've had reports of forces gathering near Calais, which certainly jibes with your hearing Folkstone."

Lynn cocked her head at Alfred. "It's as we thought. It sounds very much like they're planning an invasion."

"That's what I'm afraid of," James said. "Putting all of our intelligence together, it appears they're prepared to send forces across the Channel." He huffed a sigh and deepened his frown.

"What can we do to help?" Lynn asked, though she saw no way to do anything useful at this point.

Hamilton stood and paced to the window, where he stayed immobile.

Lynn sent a tilt of her head to Alfred, who responded with pinched lips and a shake of his head. No, give the man time.

Stuffing his hands in his pants pockets, James swiveled back to the Lunts. "Actually, there is one thing you can do."

Lynn perked up. Alfred beat her to it. "Name it," he said.

"We have a tail on those two Englishmen, guests of Bufort, that you met. We have a good idea of where they are. If you'd be willing to identify them...?"

"Of course!" they chorused together.

Lynn was skeptical. "How can that possibly help, if you know about them already?"

"Now, we have ties to those two, which needs confirmation to pick them up. If they are supposed to be helping arrange things on this side of the Channel, it may slow the Germans enough for us to react more forcefully. I think our Prime...our leaders...already have a number of offensive moves for our friends waiting in France." Hamilton strode to the door. "I need to report so we can put things in motion. Today is Thursday, yes?"

Lynn nodded. "Shall we cancel our weekend performances?"

"Absolutely not. We don't want to give anything away. Let me check with my higher-ups and get back to you on how to proceed from here. We don't want to spook them. But, then again, we don't want to wait too long either. I'll contact you again on Tuesday. By that time, we should be able to have plans in place."

"What about the other two? The other half of the Quartet?"

James took in a deep breath and pursed his lips. "They disappeared. We had them until somewhere between the train to London and its first stop. Our bet is that they slipped off the train when it slowed to shuttle onto a siding to let a troop train pass. We had good eyes on them, but..."

"You mustn't blame yourself," Alfred said. "If they are who we think they are–that is, trained Nazi infiltrators–they could probably avoid the most dogged follower."

James nodded. "I know. If they made it to the Continent, well, we don't know exactly what they would report. Hopefully, nothing crucial."

Lynn recognized stress and worry when she saw it. She went to join him at the door and set her hand on his arm. "We will help you in any way we can. You need only to call on us. And don't worry about our schedules. We can postpone anything. This is far too important to ignore."

Hamilton nodded, his hand already on the doorknob. "We will need you, I can guarantee that. I'll meet you here on Tuesday then. Look for me early afternoon, if all goes according to plan."

Alfred rose and joined him at the door. "We are at your service."

Hamilton's eyebrows pulled down and he chewed on his lip. "This is of upmost importance. Top secret, you understand? You were cleared for top secret info, and I hope you appreciate that none of this, none of it, is to be shared with anyone. Understood?"

"Of course, absolutely," Alfred said.

"Our lips are sealed," Lynn added.

"Be sure to remember that." James gave them a tight nod of his head and a quick salute, and left.

Alfred closed the door behind him. "Well, Lynnie. We're beyond simple volunteering and stage performances now."

-27-

The weekend flew by, what with multiple performances of *There Shall Be No Night* and visits and interviews. Lord Bufort did not make an appearance at any of their shows. Which was suspicious enough in itself to alert Lynn and Alfred to the importance, and perhaps the necessity for speed, over the next few days or weeks. It put them on high alert. But nothing further seemed to develop.

Monday the theater was dark, and Lynn and Alfred spent the day in what looked like their usual activities, although Lynn felt the knot in her stomach tighten as the day went on. Getting a note from James Hamilton postponing their meeting to Thursday didn't help her nerves any.

Three days to carry on. Matinees and evening performances, of course, but in between all that, Alfred returned to his hospital duties as a volunteer orderly delivering meal trays, making beds, and emptying bedpans. Lynn did duty as an air raid warden when she could. She watched searchlights sweeping the skies, finally meeting in a V to highlight a helpless silver butterfly, as she called it, summarily brought down by the ack-acks. The women working the gun emplacements to track and set the angles for the men gunners impressed her with their determination, teamwork, and professionalism.

Tuesday flowed into Wednesday, and Lynn became more and more apprehensive. She was convinced what she and Alfred found pointed most definitively to a German invasion of England. Or was it something else? She couldn't pin down her speculations. By Thursday, she was thoroughly agitated. Only Alfred was privy to her concerns.

"What if we didn't discover enough? Or anything of importance?" Lynn asked, not really expecting an answer from Alfred. She slid her hand into the crook of Alfred's elbow. They were walking along the Thames, trying not to let the rubble and the damaged skyline pull them down into a deep well of depression.

"Don't think like that, Lynnie." He reached across to shelter her hand with his. "We did the best we could. We'll know more this afternoon, when we meet with James."

Lynn sighed and murmured, "June first, 1944 today. Who knew we would be here, under such withering nightly fire, so long into the year? Seven months, so far. Still..."

Alfred squeezed her hand. "Yes, we'll stay the course. We can't put a final date on it, surely. If it takes five years, ten, we'll stay."

Tilting her head up, she smiled at her husband. "I know, darling. And we've been very lucky. Antoinette has been out of the city working with the Land Girls. She's safe, safer than here in London."

"We've been lucky here in the city, knock on wood, though we've had some close calls." Alfred chuckled. "I'd bet, some of those girls sent out to work or reclaim land have never seen a farm, and certainly never worked on one. Sometimes, I wish I could be out there helping Tony. I am a reputable farmer, after all."

Lynn laughed. "You can make me feel so much better. Antoinette would certainly be able to use your expertise. You grow the most wonderful things back home at Ten Chimneys." A moment was given over to nostalgia for what they left behind. Then she pulled herself back to the present. "But we do what we can to help raise the morale in London."

"An important job as well, Lynnie, as you know." Alfred pulled her to a stop. "We should probably start back. Time for a quick lunch along the way?"

"Sounds wonderful. Wherever we can find a small place still open."

"Then back to the hotel to meet Hamilton. I hope he has something of substance to tell us."

They stopped to take a last look at the Thames, flowing, as it always did, impassive, eternal, on its way to the sea.

***

James Hamilton did indeed have something of substance to tell them. In fact, he was almost vibrating as he rushed into their suite early in the afternoon. "Sit down, please," he said. Not much of a preamble.

Lynn recognized his focus. She led Alfred from the window to the couch and sat them both down. "You look driven. Tell us what you found."

James paced from window to sofa and back again as he spoke. "Your photo of the map, together with what you overheard, along with our own bits and pieces, has firmed up our suspicions. The Germans are gathering at Calais..." He hesitated. "It looks like to cross the Channel and invade at Folkstone. And if it's not that, then...well, who knows what they are planning."

Lynn stiffened and grasped Alfred's hand, but kept silent, knowing not to interrupt the flow of Hamilton's revelations.

"What we need now, from you two, is a definite identification of those two Brits. Our informants found that the two Germans–you were right Lynn, they were not French or Swiss–the two Germans managed to elude capture and escape back across the Channel. According to spotters, a boat, disguised as a fishing boat, spirited them away before we could apprehend them."

Alfred shook his head. "A shame. I hoped you could grab them."

James waved his hand back and forth. "They're not the problem. Whatever knowledge they pass on will be probably more affirmation of what the Germans already know." He rubbed his chin and turned to gaze out the window before turning back to them. "They know that Folkstone is a good choice. They know that there will be people on this side of the Channel who will welcome any invasion. That kind of thing." He gaze flitted back and forth, not landing on them.

Lynn recognized the signs of, if not a total lie, at least an attempt to deflect. She chose to set it aside for the moment. "What about the Brits? David and Alec, wasn't it, Alfred?" At her husband's nod, Lynn went on. "You said you needed us to identify them?"

"Yes. They are slippery characters, usually staying in the shadows. But you saw them, and heard them, at Forest Hall. All of that is enough to charge them with sedition, if not outright treason."

"What do we need to do?" Alfred asked.

"We have people on them. From what we see, they are set to leave London and head south to the coast. It's critical to get them in custody before they can do more damage. Luckily, most of May has been relatively quiet from air raids. Gives us a lull to concentrate on..." James sat down opposite them, leaning forward and fixing them with a strong gaze. He didn't finish that thought, but veered off in another direction. "I'll take you two with me. We must leave soon. Headquarters wants to give them enough leeway to send a radio message, which, with our help, will contain false information on troop movements."

Lynn sat up, raised her eyebrows, and opened her mouth to take in a great breath. Ah! Here was the road to the truth. "I see."

Alfred shared a glance with her. "I know what you're thinking Lynnie, and I think you're right on the mark."

"We've got to move now," James said, clearly ignoring them both. "There's a car waiting for us, but we have to get to it. Go, put on your uniforms. They may be Camp Show uniforms, but they'll work well enough to convince people that you are under the aegis of the regular army."

Lynn and Alfred stood, aware from Hamilton's strong language that this was not a time to pursue an explanation. That could come later. He needed them to move, and move now. They dashed to the bedroom to change.

Lynn fastened her skirt and reached for her jacket. "It's not about the coming here, Alfred. It's about going there." She turned to rummage in the armoire for her hat, and, as a result, only caught Alfred's "high tide," but missed the rest of what he said.

No time to ask, as James was hollering, "Let's go! Now! Move!" and varieties of the same sentiment.

* * *

Hamilton drove like the Furies were on his tail. No official driver this time, just James and the two of them in a jeep headed for… They had no idea. They weren't briefed on that yet. Clearly, they were going southeast, toward the coast. No stops for villages, no slowdowns for heaven or hell. So far, they didn't hit anything…or anyone.

Lynn held on for dear life as James took corners with barely a decrease in speed. She crouched forward, hands gripping like talons onto the backs of the two front seats. In spite of that, she noticed the many troops, trucks, and myriad of army vehicles they encountered. This, as she remembered, wasn't really new. As soon as the weather showed any sign of lack of rain, it seemed that the military was on the move. Sometimes going south, sometimes northwest, more often, too many destinations to draw any firm conclusions.

With a canvas top and no doors to speak of, any attempt at conversation, even if she shouted, would be whipped away by the wind. She tried anyway. "Where are we going?"

James, apparently more accustomed to deciphering words through the maelstrom of wind and road noise, answered, "Hastings."

How appropriate. The locus for the Norman invasion in 1066. Now, would this be the weak site for the Germans to exploit for an invasion in 1944? Or...? The jeep gave a jolt as it rumbled across a rough spot in the road. No point in asking more questions. James needed to be left alone to drive, if driving was what this mad dash could be called.

As they neared the coast, they encountered more traffic. More traffic in the form of trucks of all kinds, but dominated by military vehicles. James swerved off to a side road, but it proved almost as clogged. Lynn surmised that he must have more than a passing knowledge of the terrain in this part of England.

Finally, after turning into more and more narrow lanes, they appeared to reach some kind of destination, though they were still nowhere near the coast. A cluster of buildings huddled under trees next to a wide swath of field. Buildings there to house farm equipment, perhaps, considering the field was showing signs of plantings making their way to the surface in the warm June afternoon.

James pulled up next to a barnlike structure. "Time to get some answers. Come on, let's go in. They're waiting for us."

They? Lynn exchanged a puzzled look with Alfred, but he only shrugged. No idea from that quarter either. They clambered out of the jeep and followed James. Lynn pulled off her gloves as she walked. Even with leather gloves, her hands were fiery red from the exertion of hanging on. Her excitement and apprehension kept her hands trembling a bit. She stuffed her gloves into a pocket and entered the barn, passing the men as James held open the door for her.

Not one of the dozen or so men scattered at tables so much as flinched, once they took an initial look as Hamilton led them deeper into the building. A man in uniform standing in the doorway of a room built into a corner waved them over. They made their way into the small room with a man sitting ramrod straight at a desk that spoke of serious business, what with papers stacked along the sides and what looked like a map in front of the occupant. The door closed behind the three of them.

The General–that is what Lynn discerned he was, from the two stars on his shoulder–arose from the desk and reached across to shake hands with James. "Hamilton. Glad to see you were able to run the gauntlet. Roads pretty clogged." He indicated three chairs opposite him. "Sit. We have some time before you need to leave. Let's see what you've got."

James cleared his throat, and glanced at the Lunts.

The General waved his hand. "Don't worry. They gave them clearance again before you sent them in. Go on."

Lynn almost missed the next exchange. Clearance? So, they, whoever in the government "they" was– James was speaking.

"Well, sir, the Lunts here were able to ascertain..." He went on to summarize their foray into Bufort's study, where they found the map, and their nighttime reconnaissance of the greenhouse. He still didn't introduce their host.

Lynn didn't ask. Better not to tread on ground that was mined. If they wanted to give names, they would. She slid back in her chair and waited. They would be called on in due time.

"We got the film developed," the General said, "and it confirms what we suspected. There is a huge buildup of troops and equipment around Calais. Once we deciphered the columns of numbers, many of the numbers correspond to German units."

"One more thing, sir," James said. "May I?" He tipped his head at Lynn and Alfred.

The General nodded.

"Lynn, before we left in such a hurry, you said you saw something. What did you see?"

"I didn't say I saw something, exactly. What I meant was that I understood something. Well, at least, I think I understand something." She glanced at Alfred.

"Go ahead, darling. I concur with your conclusions."

The General sat forward, settled his elbows on his desk and tented his hands in front of his face. His eyebrows shifted upward and shallow ridges rose on his forehead.

Lynn skooched to the front of her chair and set one hand on the edge of the desk, turning so she had the three men in her sightline. "You led us to believe that what we found was a plan for an invasion by the Germans, an invasion across the Channel, perhaps from Calais to Folkstone. Based on what we found, as well as what we heard, that was the conclusion."

"That's right," Alfred said. "We saw the lines on the map going from France to the southeast coast here. We heard 'Folkstone' and 'France' and 'troops', and that seemed to fit the bill." A graceful movement of his arm indicated to Lynn to go on.

"But while it was all about movements, it wasn't about German troops going from France to England, was it?"

The General pursed his lips behind his fingers, but said nothing. He exchanged a glance with Hamilton that said much more, a glance that told Lynn she was on the right track.

"It's really about Allied troops going from England to France." She sat back in her chair again. "Are we right?"

The General slid back in his seat, hands now clasped in his lap, as if protecting something precious. His chest swelled as he took in a very deep breath and held it.

-28-

Lynn reached across the gap between their chairs, and met Alfred's hand coming to meet hers. They clasped hands and waited.

"Well?" Alfred said. "We're right, aren't we? We've been hearing for months about a troop buildup, and saw it with our own eyes when we were on the train down to Forest Hall, and even more so on the drive back to London."

"There is a strong feeling that we must get onto the Continent in order to win this war," Lynn said. "We can't allow Hitler to invade England, even though he planned to do just that in 1940. This is the last bastion, and we cannot hold out forever. That means going to them." She sounded like many in England, even the most humble citizens. Allied raids into Germany to drop bombs could only do so much. Russia was poised on the Eastern Front. Italy was subdued and Mussolini powerless. The weather was getting better. What better time to try for a foothold? But where? And when? That Lynn didn't know.

The General and James still sat silent. The General's forehead ridges subsided. The General asked, "Do you have more speculations?"

Lynn recognized the slight decrease in tension. The wariness was gone.

Alfred smiled. "Now, these are quite purely speculations, but informed ones, I think. Lynn and I haven't had time to really talk these over." He turned to her and squeezed her hand. "Feel free to add anything, darling."

"Thank you," she said. "I'm interested to see if we align."

"So," Alfred began, "we're not talking about the Germans invading England. We're talking about the Allies invading the Continent. How am I doing so far?"

The other two could sub for the stone lions in front of the British Museum, they sat so still. Nary a whisker-twitch.

"If that is indeed the case, then the question remains, when and where."

Lynn took over. "A beach is far more accommodating than a cliff, so that means rising tide is the best bet for getting massive numbers of troops on beaches."

"And when is high tide?" Alfred asked, then answered his own question before anyone could respond. Although, it looked as if they weren't going to get any response anyway. "A decent high tide occurs during a full moon, even I know that. So, gentlemen, when is the next full moon?"

Lynn suspected that, from the gleam in his eye and one corner of his mouth uplifted, Alfred already knew the answer. But she waited. Alfred waited. They heard murmurs, clicks, static, from the men in the outer room. Still, they waited.

James shifted in his seat and uncrossed his arms. He looked to the leader in the room, the man behind the desk, then turned to Lynn and Alfred. "We are not at liberty to say."

The General tented his fingers in front of his lips again, and tilted his head to look down at his desk.

"Sunday," Alfred said. "The next full moon is Sunday."

"*This* Sunday?" Lynn was dismayed. Sure enough, Alfred already checked. "That's only three days away!" She lifted her index finger to the General, as if ready to accuse. She thought better of it and tucked her hand into her lap. But she still wanted to know. "If you are indeed–"

"We cannot divulge anything. We have eyes on Alec Portnoy and David Stuart. You identify them when they send their radio message, and we can arrest them for treason." The General stopped.

Alfred said, "Your silence on the matter is enough to ensure that the Allies are planning on landing on a French beach somewhere, probably Monday, considering there's a full moon, ensuring a very decent high tide. If the goal is Calais, then I wonder if we did enough. The Channel is narrow there, so it's a natural spot. But the Germans seem to be fortified to meet any assault, based on what we found, and what we heard."

The General ignored them, and focused on James Hamilton. "Get these two over to Folkstone, so we can get those men apprehended. Once we get a definitive identification, then we are in the clear. Just make sure the radio operator listening doesn't send in the troops too soon. We need hard evidence of a transmission that will trap them."

"Yes, sir," James said. "I'll bring them back here when–"

The General was shaking his head before Hamilton finished. "No. I need you to check out the...." He flapped his hand, as if Hamilton would understand his meaning. "Explain only what's necessary. Report as soon as Portnoy and Stuart are in custody. Take only the authorized roads. You might make better time. Dismissed."

James stood, saluted, and herded the Lunts out of the room and back to the jeep. "Ready? I'll get you back to London once you've finished your mission. Then we can hand off the rest to the next team."

Lynn thought it best to take direction without any attempt to divert James from his orders. From what was not said, even more than from what was said, she knew this was a crucial time. For months, movements in and out of London, full trains and trucks even out in the country, presaged some momentous push. It was as if the entire land was inhaling, gathering strength for a great blast aimed at the Continent. Everyone knew that England the island couldn't hold out forever. Troops needed to land on French soil in order to push east and... She couldn't bear to predict, for fear of jinxing the operation. The only thing she hoped was that Calais was not the intended spot.

Soon, they were jostling along the "authorized roads," which turned out to be mainly country lanes and small feeder roads. No major arteries. In spite of that, the roads were clogged with troops, trucks, artillery, and other jeeps. The movements seemed willy-nilly and frantic at first, but Lynn discerned a pattern and a determined pace. It sealed her conviction that Churchill and Eisenhower were getting closer and closer to invading.

The roads were crammed with vehicles, sometimes so many that some were pulled off onto the verge, waiting for the chance to join the flow, or just parked in neat rows, as if waiting for drivers. This time of year, early June, Mother Nature provided plenty of leafy cover, and at each opportunity, the area was packed with trucks, ambulances, jeeps, tanks, armored cars. Even private gardens and dead-end lanes held piles of armaments, rations, tires, timber, more. Most of this was hidden from observation from above. Along the road, men marching, men packed into trucks, men setting up camp, men working on vehicles. Lynn even spotted a group of soldiers in a field playing cricket.

When she saw a line of ambulances along the verge, her shoulders tightened. Visions of ambulances weaving through the streets of London. Alfred would see even more, working as an orderly at a hospital. But now, these were ambulances going out, not coming back. Going out empty to be filled with wounded and dead troops. No, not troops. Soldiers. People. Soft, vulnerable people. Men whose bodies might not be able to contain the assaults made upon them. Her mind filled with bodies on beaches, in fields, along roadways, moaning, bleeding, reaching. Or worse. Still, quiet, the spirit fled.

She closed her eyes and shook her head to loosen the sights and put them into a corner. Once thought, once seen, they could not be unseen. But they could be contained, to be brought out only when she willed it. That was the hope, anyway.

Lynn brought gratitude to the fore. She gave thanks for the horde–no, not horde, she corrected herself–a great host gathering for what was obviously going to be a massive operation. She added thanks for the trees and hedges camouflaging these forces. Nibbling at the edge of her thoughts, however, were Lord Bufort's minions. How much did they know? All of what was going on could not be completely concealed. There was simply too much, too many troops gathering, too much of everything to ignore. A person would have to be blind.

Only the when, and hopefully the where, might remain unknown. But how long could that remain secret? Lynn knew the Allies would have taken precautions, steps, efforts to mask those two crucial marks. When. Where. She hoped with a fervent heart that what she and Alfred discovered was another firm cog in helping the Allies. The map showed Calais. Were the Allies planning on crossing to Calais? That way lay madness. Too many German troops stationed there.

No, not Calais. But perhaps that was what was implied. That the Germans would read it as the true landing zone. Lynn's head felt ready to explode. Never had she been part of a scene where she did not have total control. Here, neither she nor Alfred was the director of the action on this vast stage. She must get control of her thoughts, at least, or she would be overwhelmed. The traffic was thick enough that James was reduced to a less frantic pace, enough to allow Lynn to slide back in the seat and set herself the task of deep breathing and keen observation, without thinking herself into a hole.

As they got closer to Folkstone, James had to slow the jeep to a crawl. Too much traffic and materiel clogging the road and even the verges. Once around a bend, the saw the reason. A contingent of much larger armaments was being deployed, setting up in a huge field and along the tree line. Tanks, cannons, jeeps, and trucks were scattered across the grounds, and personnel of all kinds, even civilians, by the looks of things.

Lynn couldn't believe her eyes. "Look!" She stretched her arm out and pointed. "An airplane! What on earth...?"

"Look there, Lynnie." Alfred's voice betrayed an incredulity as deep as hers. "I don't believe what I'm seeing."

Lynn swiveled to align her gaze with his. She squinted, sure she couldn't be seeing what she...was seeing. Yes, Alfred was right. Unbelievable. "What is going on, James? There's a tank that...appears to be emerging from the ground. It's flat! But it's expanding. What?"

"All right, old man," Alfred said. "This deserves some kind of explanation."

They came to a standstill in the crush of vehicles and men. "Yes, an explanation. "I'm sorry we couldn't give you more before we sent you out, but we needed you to gather information without a preconception of what we were looking for. You might have missed something otherwise. As for this..." He cleared his throat and sneaked a glance at both of them. "Now's as good a time as any." He turned in the seat, set one arm on the steering wheel and gave them a crooked smile. "This, needless to say, is Top Secret."

Lynn leaned forward from the back seat, on high alert once more. Alfred patted James's knee. "Of course," they chimed together.

"What you see here is the Ghost Army. And you're right, it looks like it's growing out of the ground. That's because these divisions are inflatable." He waited a moment.

Lynn looked at her husband. "It's all right here, out in the open. No attempt to conceal."

"Of course," Alfred said. "Decoys."

"Exactly," James said. "Decoys. They can be moved rather quickly, though it takes time to deflate them. Still, they can be deployed much faster than a real division of artillery. A few days ago, they were a bit farther down the coast, but with the information you brought, they are now here, close to Folkstone."

"So, even if the Germans were attempting a landing here, perhaps the Ghost Army would deter them," Alfred said. "But we know–"

James intervened. "Feints and decoys and plenty of false information has been seeping out, keeping the Germans off balance, guessing. Everybody knows we have to make landfall over there." They all knew what "over there" meant. "We've even tried feeding Lord Haw-Haw bits and pieces. With that traitor broadcasting from Germany, he can't be sure of the details of what's going on over here. But he's so violently anti-British–"

"But he's British himself, isn't he?" Alfred asked.

"Not really. Irish, but he has a British passport," Hamilton said. "If I could get my hands on him..."

Lynn said, "We're here trying to boost morale, and he's on the radio quipping, 'Germany calling, Germany calling' in that snide mocking tone." She pushed her hand off to the side, as if ridding herself of the odious turncoat.

"Well, he doesn't seem to be succeeding," Alfred said. "Not for the people we talk to, and we talk to plenty."

"He's got lots of listeners in England, though," James said, "even if some are listening just to hear what foolishness he's spouting now." He shook his head. "Either way, not good for morale."

"It's clear the Germans aren't planning on coming, from what I see." Lynn brought them back around to the Ghost Army and its purpose. "It's just the opposite. It isn't about them coming in. It's about the Allies going out." She tapped her forehead with an index finger, and winked. "This Ghost Army is designed to draw them closer to Calais, so they won't be close to where the Allies will actually be landing. It's a wonderful piece of stagecraft, isn't it Alfred? Worthy of the best faux stage sets we've ever produced."

"So, when is this massive operation to take place? And where?" Alfred said, probing, though Lynn knew it was rather futile.

James was silent for a blink. "That is above my pay grade to know, or even to disclose if I did know." The road congestion eased, and he turned back to maneuver through, past the Ghost Army's feverish preparations going on in the field.

His silence on the matter was enough to convince Lynn that she and Alfred were spot-on about an operation designed to put forces on the Continent. Of course, with all the buildup in England, almost anybody could see at least that much. She squeezed Alfred's shoulder, then slid back against her seat, satisfied they had a more complete picture of things. She amended herself. Not nearly complete, but it would have to suffice, until the start of...whatever it was, was announced publicly.

The roadway was finally clear enough to maintain a reasonable pace, and the three of them settled into a silence. A tense silence, but no longer a silence lacking clarity and purpose.

Before long, they were ensconced in a Folkstone hotel manager's office, peering out through a crack in the door as patrons, mostly military men, checked in at the reception desk or hurried across the lobby heading who knows where. The city, so close to the beleaguered Continent across the Channel, was almost totally destroyed over the course of several years. From local reports, the population dropped to almost half of its previous numbers, both from deaths and from people abandoning their devastated homes and city. Even the hotel where James and the Lunts waited was damaged. Sandbags and jury-rigged repairs to walls and windows made the place look like something out of a Gothic horror story.

Perhaps, Lynn thought, that was the point of choosing this particular location for a surreptitious, and seditious, radio transmission to German-held territory in France. Who would believe that the enemy was within these damaged walls?

Alfred, positioned to see a portion of the entrance to the hotel, elbowed Lynn. She shifted to scrunch below him and share his angle. Yes, here they came. Portnoy and Stuart. She reached out, found James Hamilton's knee, and squeezed. No need for words.

"Are you sure?" James's whisper was grainy enough to indicate concern.

"Those two in tweed trousers and khaki trench coats are David Stuart and Alec Portnoy. Stuart is the one in the green watch cap. Portnoy is carrying a maroon suitcase. Will that do?" Alfred and Lynn moved back, and James closed the door.

"Quite so," James said. "Stay here. I'll give the go-ahead to the radio team. Then we'll get you out of here."

Lynn rocked out of a squat and levered herself off the floor. She joined Alfred in front of the damaged fireplace of the manager's office. "I didn't expect that to be so easy."

James returned to their side. "It's not over yet. The radio team needs to hear and record the beginning of the transmission. That will be the nail in the coffin. We'll wait to hear they've actually got that. We'll make sure they're marched out by the military police, and then we can leave. Once I report back, I'll drive you up to London."

"At night?" Lynn asked. "Is that safe?"

"Should we bunk down somewhere?" Alfred asked.

James shook his head. "It's safer to get you out of the line of fire down here. We can be back at the Savoy soon after midnight. Hopefully, we can all get a good night's sleep. The weekend is going to be...rather busy."

Lynn smiled. "Understood. So, we won't be seeing you for a while then." It wasn't even a hint of a question.

James sent them a crooked smile. "Not a chance."

The beginning of the end, Lynn thought, and crossed her fingers.

-29-

The weekend was indeed busy. The Lunts were committed to providing distractions to the populace, and to themselves, by performances all weekend, including a matinee on Saturday, as well as an evening performance. The blackout curfew was still enforced, so they were out of the theater and back at the Savoy shortly after nine o'clock. But that only afforded more time for worry and speculation. But they quashed any speculation, knowing it would be fruitless. They knew forces were poised to leave England, though they didn't know from where exactly.

They knew the full moon on Sunday and Monday nights would provide plenty of light as ships made their way across the Channel. With a vast armada–Lynn imagined a carpet of ships, not a scattering–moonlight would help ships avoid each other in the night. Probably even more important, the full moon would create a full incoming tide, allowing ships and landing craft to get close to the beach.

All of these things Lynn and Alfred hashed over, again and again, until they realized that the best thing they could do would be to give the best stage performances they could. That was one way to help the people focus away from the troop movements they lived with for the past several months. Would it be tonight? No, not possible.

Look how calm the Lunts carry on. Of course, they know no more than we do. The crisis is coming...but not today. Surely, not today.

By Sunday evening, with the matinee over and their evening free, the Lunts decided to eat dinner in public. Lynn felt it was one of their best performances. Stroll calmly, arm in arm. Ponder the menu, little fingernail tucked between her teeth, a classic theater move. Lift a glass of wine. Laugh, linger over the food. Debate over indulging in dessert. Another glass of wine. Or perhaps port. Finish the evening ensconced in the Savoy bar, blackout curtains in place, lighting subtle and low, long after the curfew hour.

Midnight found them back in their room. But unable to settle, or go to bed.

Lynn shivered. "Alfred, I just felt...something. A quiver, a shake, something. Do you see anything?"

Alfred came from the window to sit beside her on the sofa. "No. But there might be something going on. Tonight, the moon is full."

"What if..." She couldn't voice more.

"Don't. Don't think about it. We can do nothing, truly."

She turned a stricken face to him. "We should turn on the radio. Won't they...announce...if anything?"

"Good idea, Lynnie." Alfred got up and strode across the room. "I'll get the BBC."

"I think they've signed off for the night, Alfred."

Out of character, with a crackle and a burst of static, the radio sprang to life. *...out of Wales. Raining in sheets. Irish weather watchers warn to batten down the hatches. It's going to be a wild weather night in London. That ends our coverage for...*" Alfred turned off the radio.

Lynn frowned. "Something is happening. They're not usually on this late. Although the weather is... No, that's actually good news for the citizens, because the German bombers won't be able to come across. And..." She sent a sudden stricken look to Alfred.

Alfred pursed his lips. "That might put a damper on everything."

"Oh, Alfred, when we checked on the nights of full moons, the next one is in July. By that time, the Germans may be able to ferret out what is really happening. How can we keep all of those troops and...and...stuff secret for another month?"

Alfred went to Lynn, sat down, and gripped her hands in both of his. "We can only watch and listen. If not tonight, then maybe tomorrow. You know they're keeping a close eye on every single thing that could cause a change in plans."

Lynn could almost feel him holding back the words "abort the mission." "Tomorrow the theater is dark. We must spend the time keeping busy. You go to the hospital, as usual. And I'll join the women at the Red Cross."

"Good idea, Lynnie." Alfred kissed her fingers. "Right now, I propose we go to bed." He stood and pulled her up.

She nestled into his chest. "Just hold me for a moment, darling. Then it's off to bed."

* * *

Monday turned out to be one of those normal days, if there were such a thing during a raging war. No morning BBC radio reports about an invasion of the Continent. Nothing at all about Allied troop movements, of course. Only rather ordinary reports about German sallies. Lynn wondered if the soldiers they saw along the roads were demoted to meaningless cricket games while they waited for orders.

Alfred and Lynn dressed, turned off the radio, and went down for breakfast. They dallied over the buffet in the Savoy dining room, hoping to hear what Eisenhower had up his sleeve. But the Supreme Allied Commander was silent. Lynn wondered where he was at the moment. With the moon following only its own orders, Lynn knew time might be running out.

Of course, she and Alfred could be wrong. She shook her head. They saw too much. Everything pointed to a go very soon. She frowned and put her hands over her ears for a moment to retreat into herself.

Alfred touched her shoulder. "Time to go, Lynnie. We've got to keep ourselves busy, or I'm going to explode." He was already standing, and he offered the crook of his elbow.

"My thoughts exactly. I'm taking off my worry clothes, and putting on my work clothes. Just like the theater. We can do this." She took his arm and they made their way out of the hotel.

Lynn spent the day helping at the Red Cross, while Alfred continued his work as orderly at the hospital. They ate lunch with the locals they were working with, and met only for the evening meal.

The radio was on at Lynn's worksite, and she kept one ear tuned to weather reports that came on hourly. The skies seemed to be clearing by afternoon, but the reporters warned of high seas still on the Irish Sea and on the English Channel. With every report, Lynn's hands slowed at whatever she was doing, and she held her breath. She forced herself to keep a placid face, and engage fully in conversations going on around her.

By the time the afternoon was over, she was exhausted.

-30-

Monday midnight found Lynn standing at the window, peering between the blackout curtains to assess the level of moonlight. She strained to see across the miles to the harbors, breakwaters, and beaches of England's south coast. Impossible, of course, but she squinted and searched anyway.

She heard Alfred get out of bed and shuffle up behind her. She leaned into his chest as his arms went around her. "Where, where, where? Do you think they've begun?"

Alfred sighed, making the hair over her ear flutter. "Impossible to tell, Lynnie. Come back to bed."

"I wish we could get in touch with James." She puffed out a breath. "It would be no use, I know. He's far too busy to think of two nervous Nellies. But still..."

Alfred walked her backwards toward the bed, his arms still around her.

She took a last look toward the window, then allowed herself to be drawn to bed. How could she possibly sleep when thoughts of all those boys heading eventually for France swirled through her head. How many would come back? How many would be lost on the beaches, in the towns, along the roads? It was unthinkable. Overwhelming. She cuddled closer to Alfred.

In spite of her conviction that she wouldn't sleep, she drifted in and out of dreams, dreams that morphed from benign beach scenes with children playing in the sand to red sands with soldiers holding out bloody hands while thunderheads growled and shot lightning behind them. Finally, her mind called a truce, and she descended into deep sleep.

Suddenly, she bolted upright, with no memory of what dragged her awake. But there was a feeling...

The pre-dawn light was so soft that the edges of furniture, drapes, window, sky blended into each other in shades of gray. Impossible to tell if it would be a clear day.

Alfred's eyes were still closed and his breathing even. Lynn set a hand on his shoulder.

"I'm awake, Lynnie. What is it?" He opened his eyes and set his gaze on her.

"I...I don't really know, Alfred." She swung her legs over the side of the bed and slid her feet into her mules. Eschewing her dressing gown, she went to the window and pulled aside the thick drape, not caring if anyone saw her in her nightgown. "The sun isn't up yet, but I can see a bit more as the sky lightens. Some bits of light clouds and a stiff breeze from what I can see."

Alfred padded over, stood behind her and gathered her to him.

"I just have a feeling..." Lynn leaned back against Alfred's chest. She really wished Antoinette were back in London. A selfish wish. Tony was safer out in the counties, helping the Land Girls and the farmers. She sent out some positive thoughts to her sister. They would be back together as soon as- Alfred was saying something.

"I wonder where they are now?" Alfred said. Neither one had to define what they were talking about. "I have a feeling that today is the day. Look at the weather. Yesterday was so blustery, rainy off and on all day. Not perfect conditions. Today looks a little better."

Lynn pictured the great armada of ships moving across the Channel in the dark of the night. By dawn, before the tide rose too high, she imagined the minesweepers would finish clearing the shallow waters and the deliberate German debris on the beaches. A little after dawn, if the tide were rising, they would be able to land troops–soldiers–on the beach. The sight of that line of ambulances flashed through her mind. She pushed it aside.

"This would be the best time to land," Alfred said. He squeezed her in a tight hug.

"Alfred, I simply cannot stand still one moment longer." Lynn rotated within his hug and planted her hands on his chest. "Let's get out of here and go for a walk. If today is truly the day, news won't be coming through this early. And I will simply shatter if I can't keep myself busy."

Alfred dropped his arms. "I'm with you on that. Let's go."

Lynn flicked on the lights and went to the radio. When she turned it on, static and buzzing greeted her. She dialed to the BBC, but it wasn't broadcasting yet. Lynn checked her wristwatch. "It's only six o'clock, Alfred."

"Too early," Alfred called from the bathroom.

Yes, she knew that, so she chose not to respond. She turned off the radio.

Within twenty minutes, they were moving through a fairly empty lobby. The man at the reception desk took their key with a cheery "Good morning." A waiter rushed by and on into the dining room, his white apron in place. Running a bit late, by the looks of it. Lynn knew the chef, toque perched on his head, would already be creating omelets with the Savoy eggs, or conjuring up something from whatever rations–or black market goods–he could secure. One man relaxed in a chair, legs crossed, reading a newspaper. Nothing unusual, even this early. Lynn couldn't wait to get outside.

They walked to the door, where the doorman, secure at his post, opened the door and tipped his hat. Alfred offered his elbow and Lynn slipped her hand into the crook, a comfortable fit.

"A stroll, Alfred. Nothing fast, please. No need to rush."

Alfred patted her hand and they set off, matching step for step, Alfred shortening his stride a bit to match hers. The sun was up as they set off down The Strand, skirted Trafalgar Square and headed along The Mall, with the lawns and trees of St. James Park on their left. Buckingham Palace grew larger and larger in the morning light as they drew closer. Clouds scudded across the sky, and the wind, coming out of the northwest, was cool, but not uncomfortable.

Lynn concentrated on keeping her steps even and confident. She recognized the weather, of course, but refused to meld that with what might be going on along the English coast, or on the Continent.

They circled the Victoria Memorial and headed down Birdcage Walk to Big Ben and the Thames. They walked along the river until they needed to turn away to reach the Savoy, only a block or two inland. By this time, Lynn was tired. A walk of over an hour before breakfast, before tea or scones or one of the chef's marvelous omelets, would prove exhausting for anyone. Couple that with the stretches of destruction and rubble from the bombings, and Lynn could feel that both of them were descending into emotional exhaustion as well.

The hotel lobby was busy by the time they set off across it, heading for the dining room. Lynn said, "What I wouldn't give for a nice cup of tea."

One waiter seated them, while another, like a fairy godfather, appeared at Lynn's elbow with a teapot, cup and saucer. She sent him a grateful tip of the head and smile.

Alfred was served a cup of coffee, and the waiter disappeared after taking their order. "I much prefer making my own coffee," Alfred said, whispering over the lip of his cup. "But I won't complain about this. They're lucky to get any coffee at all."

In the middle of breakfast, the hotel manager burst into the dining room, the door banging against a chair as it swung wildly open. The silence was instantaneous. This kind of interruption was unprecedented, and highly irregular.

The manager, without any warning, belted out, "Bulletin! News coming on from B–"

Lynn and Alfred didn't stop to hear the rest of his announcement, but, in one frantic motion, dropped their forks, pushed back their chairs, and made a mad dash for the lobby.

No question about it, The Day had begun. Could there be any doubt?

-31-

When they erupted into the lobby, the receptionist was snaking an extension cord across the carpet to a wall outlet. The hotel set up their big radio, now hunched closer to the center of the room. Lynn and Alfred took two chairs with a small table in front of them, as close to the radio as they could get without blocking anyone. They dropped into the chairs and reached across the gap to hold hands. All around them, people were circling, then settling wherever they could, like a whirlpool with the radio at the center. The noise, the questions, became deafening. Until the manager held up his hand for silence.

The sound level dropped instantly.

The radio was clicked on and the BBC dialed in. A bit of static, then...

8 a.m. Frederick Allen here with a special bulletin. Supreme Allied Headquarters have issued an urgent warning to inhabitants of the enemy-occupied countries living near the coast. The warning said that a new phase in the Allied Air Offense had begun. Shortly before this warning the Germans reported that Havre, Calais and Dunkirk were being heavily bombarded and that German naval units were engaged with Allied landing craft.

Murmurs flowed across the room, quickly escalating to shouted questions after the BBC announced that more bulletins would be forthcoming, but no further news was available at this time. The airwaves switched to bland music.

Lynn squeezed Alfred's hand and turned to exchange a look that said it was better to keep silent. They already knew more than the other guests in the lobby. Calais bombarded. Yet another deception. If the Germans were reporting air assault sites, then the Ghost Army did its work successfully. Lynn and Alfred's report might have helped those inflatable deployments get into place to mislead German high command. They might never know. But at this point, Lynn didn't really mind. Charities they performed offstage were private more often than not.

No one left the Savoy, and a few more people came in from the street, probably hearing there was something auspicious going on with Allied troops. Before long, waiters appeared weaving among the crowd, offering coffee or tea. Alfred managed to snag one of each, depositing the cups on the small table in front of their chairs. They sat, sipping and listening to the ebb and flow of conversation as it rose, collided with the walls, and settled back again. Others, especially those seated, mirrored their stillness, or moved enough to put heads close together for more subdued talk. Lynn and Alfred, rather isolated where they were, took in snatches of questions, mainly, and opted not to try and correct or explain the many theories being offered around them.

Lynn set her empty teacup down and turned sideways in her chair, the better to chat with Alfred. "Perhaps I should go up and get my deck of cards. A few rounds of Patience might help calm my nerves as we wait for more news."

"Solitaire always settles you before a performance, Lynnie. That sounds like a good idea," Alfred said. "But you sit tight. I'll run up and get your cards. I think I'll grab a morning newspaper as well. I'll be–"

Before he had a chance to reassure her of his quick return, the radio sprang to life once more. The music, which apparently faded into the background for most listeners in the room, stopped like a child silenced by a parent. The volume of "Here is a special bulletin, read by John Snagge," quieted everyone.

Lynn glanced at her wristwatch. Noon. She reached for Alfred's hand again. Midday. They must be on the beaches by now. Inadvertently, without warning, the scene she so carefully packed away came to life. Clouds roiling in the sky, rollers of water sweeping up from landing craft. Men, perhaps up to their thighs in water, holding guns aloft, pouring out and slogging up from water to sand. As much as she knew that those ambulances would be filled before this day was over, she tried not to imagine the sight of bullets flying, finding purchase in chests, legs, arms...heads. She kept the scene in black and white, like the newsreels, knowing the color of blood seeping everywhere would do her in. Likewise, the scene remained silent in her mind. She knew the sounds of incoming bombs, explosions in the air, crackling fires and booms of falling buildings. But she could not transfer that to the all-too human carnage sure to be going on at those French beaches. Even the cries of those who suffered the London bombardments would not be equal. The sight in her mind would be more than enough.

John Snagge came on.

D-day has come. Early this morning the Allies began the assault on the north-western face of Hitler's European Fortress. The first official news came just after half-past nine when Supreme Headquarters of the Allied Expeditionary Force said: "Under the Command of General Eisenhower, Allied Naval Forces supported by strong Air Forces, began landing Allied Armies this morning on the northern coast of France." It was announced a little later that General Montgomery is in command of the Army Group carrying out the assault. This Army Group includes Canadian and United States Forces.

Though Snagge continued to report, a cry of triumph from the Savoy hotel lobby rolled up the stairs and even out into the street.

The manager raised his hands, as he did earlier, and, without a word, everyone complied. Silence.

Snagge's voice again.

...Eisenhower said: The tide has turned. We will accept nothing less than full victory.

Full victory. Lynn took in a deep breath. That was still a long way off. As far as anyone knew, the Allies had only a mere toehold on the coast, not even a foothold. Although, news would take time to reach them here in London, so perhaps the forces already moved off the beaches and into the fields. She fervently hoped that was true.

After Snagge signed off, the regular radio announcer added that BBC correspondents were with the forces, even as they crossed the Channel. BBC hoped to have firsthand reports from the front, and would pass them along as soon as they could.

Music again.

Now, more coffee, more tea, sometimes handed from guest to guest, as the press of people in the lobby reached a density prohibiting proper service from the kitchen and wait staff. No one seemed to mind.

1 p.m. Another bulletin. *Allied troops were landed under strong naval and air cover on the coast of Normandy early this morning.*

Lynn grabbed both of Alfred's hands and leaned so close their noses almost touched. "Normandy! Of course, Alfred! Think of those crescents of beaches stretching for miles along the coast. Perfect! Calais may be closer, but Eisenhower chose well."

"I'm sure it was a group effort. A decision that big takes Americans, English, Canadians, who knows who else. You're right, of course, Normandy presents a much longer front," Alfred said. "A lot better than Calais." They turned back to the radio.

...beach landing still going on at midday, and mass airborne landings successfully made behind enemy lines. More than four-thousand ships, and several thousand smaller craft, have crossed the Channel; and some eleven-thousand first-line aircraft can be drawn upon for the battle.

Details arrived sporadically, more often by rumor and speculation than by the BBC. Alfred finally peeled himself away from the press to go up their suite and get Lynn's deck of cards. On the way back, he grabbed a morning newspaper from the stack on the reception desk. Nothing of an invasion via Normandy there, of course. Everyone knew, even the Germans, that a landing on the Continent was coming. They probably had the date narrowed down within a handful of days as well. That had everyone holding their breath. But none of that would appear in any newspaper.

Lynn laid out a hand of Patience and played it as far as she could. She shuffled the cards and laid out another. And another. And yet another. The afternoon wore on. Alfred made his way around the lobby, joining first this group, then that, more, Lynn thought, to keep himself occupied while the clock kept a snail's pace tracking the time.

The crowds thinned as people left to go home, to locate a friend or relative to visit, or to find a pub to share a pint and listen to the BBC a bit more comfortably.

Alfred returned to her side eventually. Lynn lost track as she tried to concentrate on the cards. "What do you say, Lynnie? Shall we put in an order for a room service dinner, something simple? We can listen to the King's speech at nine o'clock even better upstairs. More peace and quiet."

Lynn suddenly realized just how tired she was. The past few days drained her, though she could put up a good front. She allowed her shoulders to slump just a little before she buoyed herself upright again. "Oh, my dear, that sounds simply divine. I don't mind sharing with the crowds, but our part of the performance is as good as over. I'd be quite happy to slip away."

Alfred offered his hand. She gathered up her cards and slipped her hand in his, feeling his strength making its way from his fingers to hers. She lifted her chin and stood up.

"I'll call down for room service a bit later," Alfred said. "Looks like the reception desk is busy right now." He slipped his arm across her waist.

"Thank you, my dear," Lynn said. "I am ready to reacquaint myself with my nightgown."

-32-

Well before nine o'clock, Lynn was curled next to Alfred, with him propped on a pair of plump pillows. The radio was earlier moved closer to the bed, in order to catch anything of importance, while they waited for the King's speech.

"I'm glad we canceled tonight's performance," Lynn said. "Everyone wanted to keep abreast of the situation. No one wanted to be in the theater."

"Like us, they're probably all still glued to the radio."

Lynn shifted closer, fitting herself into the curves of his body. "I don't know if I can stay awake for the King's speech. I don't want to move an inch."

Alfred, his arm under her shoulder, snugged her in closer. "Here comes something from the Prime Minister."

Lynn heard the sparkle of the radio and forced herself to pay closer attention.

Churchill reported that forces had driven several miles into France, with tough resistance in several places. Reports of air forces flooding the skies...fighters heading back to England...Flying Fortresses heading out from England...army pushed ten miles east of Caen...sandbag-weighted dummies simulating paratroopers dropped, designed to explode upon impact.

That last piece earned Alfred a gentle poke in the side and a comment. "They're still at it, Alfred. Pulling the wool over the German's eyes. But I hope everyone here understands what Churchill said, that this is a valuable and vital first step, but only a first step. There is a lot of German-held territory between the beach and Berlin."

The radio introduced King George VI, and Lynn quieted to listen. "Here's the King, Alfred," she whispered. No answer from her husband. She set her hand on his chest and felt his heart, even and steady, matching his breathing. He was asleep. *Ah, well,* she thought, *after all, this is not his king. Not totally mine anymore either, even if I do have British citizenship too.* She smiled at the thought of Alfred snubbing the king. Not intentional, certainly.

The King's voice flowed out.

Four years ago, our Nation and Empire stood alone against an overwhelming enemy, with our backs to the wall. Now once more a supreme test has to be faced.

His calm voice lulled Lynn.

...challenge...fight to win the final victory....

She closed her eyes.

Once again...we need a revival of spirit, a new unconquerable resolve...renew that crusading impulse...entered the war...pray...

Lynn caught only bits and pieces as his speech drew to a close, so exhausted was she. The last she heard were the final melodious strains of "God Save the King" as the BBC signed off for the night.

Then, silence.

Blessed, blessed silence.

AUTHOR'S NOTE

While *Shadows Behind the Scenery* is based on the events of 1943-44 in London, I took many liberties, inventing dialog, situations, and settings, including the Lunts' involvement in spying for the Allies. However, some things that seem farfetched are indeed fact. Kaspar, the famous Savoy Hotel cat, is real and still graces the lobby. The Lunts did volunteer at various jobs, one of which had Alfred emptying hospital bedpans. On a much more important scale, the real Ghost Army did exist in England in May 1944, and shortly after D-day was deployed to the Continent. A most readable source on the Ghost Army is *The Ghost Army of World War II: How One Top-Secret Unit Deceived the Enemy with Inflatable Tanks, Sound Effects and Other Audacious Fakery* (Updated Edition) by Rick Beyer and Elizabeth Sayles (2023). The account of D-day in London is as close to reality as I could make it. Thanks to the BBC's generous offer at no cost, I was able to quote from the heart-stopping transcripts of that day's real radio bulletins. The complete transcripts, riveting in their details, are available online at https://www.bbc.co.uk/programmes/articles/5jRMmQHNnXVTzfv8MCMcBdN/d-day-news-bulletins.

The Lunts stayed in London until the end of the war. They hoped to take their show to the continent once France was secured, but that was never fulfilled. Eventually, they returned to their summer estate, Ten Chimneys in Genesee Depot, Wisconsin, which has since been declared a National Historic Site, and is open to the public. Visit www.tenchimneys.org for photos, details about Lynn and Alfred, as well as information about visiting the estate. Their story continues to fascinate.

ABOUT THE AUTHOR

After earning Bachelor and Master's degrees, Mary Ann Noe spent 29 years in Waukesha classrooms, first teaching 7th grade language arts and social studies, followed by high school English and psychology. Upon retirement, she joined a writing workshop where she reinvented herself as an author. Mary Ann publishes novels through Black Rose Writing. Her non-fiction essays and poetry are in numerous print and online magazines. She spends time reading anything she can get her hands on, writing, and baking (and eating the results). Happily enjoying their grandchildren, she and her husband reside in Wisconsin, where she watches with dismay as the deer eat the flowers in the garden. Learn more at www.maryannnoe.com.

THE LYNN AND ALFRED TALE SERIES

OTHER TITLES FROM MANY ANN NOE

NOTE FROM MARY ANN NOE

Word-of-mouth is crucial for any author to succeed. If you enjoyed *Shadows Behind the Scenery*, please leave a review online—anywhere you are able. Even if it's just a sentence or two. It would make all the difference and would be very much appreciated.

Thanks!
Mary Ann Noe

We hope you enjoyed reading this title from:

BLACK ROSE writing™

www.blackrosewriting.com

Subscribe to our mailing list – *The Rosevine* – and receive **FREE** books, daily deals, and stay current with news about upcoming releases and our hottest authors.
Scan the QR code below to sign up.

Already a subscriber? Please accept a sincere thank you for being a fan of Black Rose Writing authors.

View other Black Rose Writing titles at www.blackrosewriting.com/books and use promo code **PRINT** to receive a **20% discount** when purchasing.